THE
SPACE
in
BETWEEN

a novel

Linda M. James

THE SPACE IN BETWEEN
A Novel

Copyright Linda M. James, 2017

ISBN 978-0-692-95325-9

Cover design by Rob Bignell,
Inventing Reality Editing Service

Manufactured in the United States of America
First printing October 2017

~ *Table of Contents* ~

~ *Acknowledgements* ~

First and foremost is glory to God who planted a seed in me, and then used me as a tool to grow a story that could only come from Him!

To my mother, Ruth Polz, for instilling in me a creative vision that allows me to look at the world in multiple layers of dimension. And, for encouraging me.

To my writing group who were fiercely supportive and encouraging: Aethan Hart, Bonnie Federation, Jane Nicol, Jean Krauss. My gratitude to all of you is beyond expressed words.

To Jody Eisch who nudged me by telling me that I needed to write a book. Also for being willing to read and critique the manuscript in stages as it was being written, as well as doing a final read-through. In addition, for assisting with multiple details — as my "business manager." As Henry David Thoreau said, "Friends... they cherish one another's hopes. They are kind to one another's dreams." Thank you, dear friend!

To my early readers who willingly read and made edits to my manuscript for flow, style, and grammar. Thank you Jody Eisch, Skip James, Joan Sorenson, and Molly Powers.

To my children, Ashley, Emily, and Jordan, who have always known the dream in my heart. Thank you for your encouraging words of telling me my greatest calling was to write and that I'm a dreamer. I love you.

To my extended family for believing in me.

To my sweet, funny pups, Darby Sue and Della Rose, who knew when I was working too hard and nudged my hand to stop and take time to play.

To my childhood school librarian, Mrs. Heaverlo, now deceased, who unknowingly showed me how to love words and books at a young age, even though I struggled with reading.

And to Layton "Skip" James for constant love and support. For challenging me to raise the bar and push myself. But also for believing in me no matter what! You are greatly loved.

"There is a space in between
that takes away what was
and replaces it with what is."

~ Linda M. James ~

~ *Prologue* ~

I always knew the difference between right and wrong, and good and bad. What I didn't fully understand was the unsettling feeling I had about certain things or people. It was a feeling that caused my heart to race or an uneasy pressure in my chest. I would later learn that that feeling was a warning sign.

I was a quiet and intent person, most often observing those around me. It was both a curse and a blessing. Perhaps it was a powerful sense of perception. One person who shaped my thoughts and feelings was Sally. She was bold and courageous. She was smart, but mischievous. All traits that made me uncomfortable and unable to live up to certain expectations.

That summer, 1968, was filled with both good and bad, and right and wrong. None of which I had any control, but a lot for which I felt I was to blame.

It is guilt that extinguishes all the light and breath of what has life, and it is guilt that steals the heart and soul.

~ *Chapter 1* ~

The sun was filling the room at the same time my father's booming voice was filling the stairway. "Rise and shine," he called to us every morning at the exact same time. It was the end of May, and the end of the school year.

I shared a bedroom with my sister, Sally. Her single bed was against the wall and mine was near the only window, from where I loved to look at the moon.

"Can you believe only four more days and we will be on summer vacation?" Sally asked, her voice radiant while she threw her pajamas under her pillow. She was always bright in the mornings. Within a few days time, I'd finish fourth grade and Sally would be done with sixth grade.

I didn't answer immediately as I thought about long summer days and no school schedule to keep. It was my favorite time of the year. I was always so happy when the bell rang on the very last day of school, and I was free for three months.

"Anna!" Sally yelled at me and broke my trance-like thoughts about summer. "I asked you a question!" Her voice now less cheerful.

"I know, I'm excited about summer, too," I responded.

We got dressed and made our beds before our older sister, Ellen, reminded us to get a move on if we wanted a ride from her. She warned us everyday that she would leave us behind if we weren't ready to go on time. We knew she didn't mean it. Ellen had gotten her driver's license at the beginning of the school year, and right after Christmas our father had brought home a used 1961 Ford Falcon.

"Nothing but a Ford in our driveway," my father said. He was the assistant sales manager at Springville Ford, and having a third driver in the family meant a second vehicle was needed.

Before he had handed over the keys to Ellen, my parents had sat down with her and laid out the rules. Part of the deal was to drive Sally and me to and from school every day. The only other occasion to drive the Falcon was to her job at the drugstore, where she worked as a cashier. My father made it clear that my mother also needed the car from time to time.

The Falcon was perfect for Ellen. It had four doors and was as blue as a robin's egg. The only flaws were a small tear in the backseat, and a spot of rust on the bottom of the driver's door, which looked like a ugly scab.

"Girls, hurry up, I'm leaving," Ellen threatened. As we ran out the door behind her I noticed how she was dressed. Today she was wearing a light blue sleeveless dress with a white cardigan draped over her shoulders. She smelled like a flower. And her blond, shoulder-length hair was flipped on the ends with bangs swept over to the side, complete with a white ribbon tied on top. Ellen took great care with her appearance. I figured she spent a lot of time getting ready for school so her boyfriend, Greg, would tell her how pretty she looked.

Sally and I loved to go into Ellen's room when she was gone. We'd play with her makeup and look through her clothes. Just like our bedroom, hers had a walk-in closet, which she filled with clothes she loved. When we did play in Ellen's room, Sally insisted we needed to put everything back in place so that Ellen didn't know we had been there. On more than one occasion, Ellen would grumble at us that we were not allowed in her room or in her stuff. "Leave my things alone and stay out," she warned us several times.

I wanted Ellen to understand that I simply loved looking at her grown up things, pretty clothes and her organized room, and, I just loved looking at her.

"I get the front seat!" Sally was quick to shout out every morning as we trailed Ellen to the car. "When do I get a chance in the front seat?," I asked. Of course, Sally always said the same thing, "Never, you are too little, so stop asking." Though, whenever just Ellen and I went on an errand, I was allowed to sit in the front.

I barely had climbed into the backseat when Ellen backed the car out of the driveway, and we were on our way to school. She was not one to waste a minute. The sooner she got to school the more time she had with Greg before classes.

Every school day had a similar routine, except today. After school, when Ellen picked us up, she announced that we needed to stop at the drugstore.

"You know Mom and Dad expect you to bring us right home after school," Sally said, raising her voice in annoyance. We knew our parents were strict about the rules with the car, and where we went, but today Ellen was willing to break the rules.

"It's not your concern!" Ellen was quick to counter. The two of them were never inclined to friendly conversation. They simply tolerated each other. I sat in the backseat and said nothing, just anticipating a trip to Herman's Drugstore. Ellen parked the car at an angle on Main and ordered us to stay put.

"What do you suppose she needs to buy?" Sally was curious about everything. I didn't respond to her question as I really didn't care. "Fine, don't bother to answer me," she continued in frustration.

Five minutes later Ellen came out carrying a bag, got into the Falcon, and we were on our way home. Sally immediately opened the bag to discover what the stop was all about.

"You bought a Continental Hair curling iron?" Sally seemed outraged. "That is expensive," she contested.

"What do you care? You are exactly twelve years old and you have natural curls." Ellen was irritated. "Besides I have a job and I get paid money. So there!"

Once we got home, I was quick to get out of the Falcon and up to our room where I changed clothes before heading outside. It was a beautiful day in May and I wasn't about to sit in the house.

I could hear Sally explaining to my mother that we were late because of Ellen. "I warned her that she would be in trouble if we didn't come straight home, but she wouldn't listen to me." Sally insisted that my mother impose some kind of punishment. "Plus she spent money on a curling iron. A Continental Hair curling iron. It's not cheap!" I had to admit, Sally's complaining tired me out.

"Well, you aren't terribly late and I don't need the car for any errands today so it's fine, Sally." My mother was calm. "However,

Ellen, dear, remember the rules. . . don't bend them." Ellen walked right on past and up to her room, where she closed the door behind her.

As simple as that, my mother went back to watching *The Edge of Night*, which was always on when we arrived home from school. Ellen was not in trouble for failure to drive us straight home from school, or spending money on a curling iron. After all, Ellen was almost grown up. She was nearly done with her junior year and would turn seventeen in August.

~ *Chapter 2* ~

The next morning Ellen showed up to breakfast with her hair in curls and sat down next to me. "Your hair looks nice," my father said, briefly looking up from the newspaper.

"It should look nice!" Sally exclaimed. "She spent a lot of money on a new curling iron and didn't bring us straight home after school. I think she needs to be grounded or have the car keys taken away!"

"Shut up, Sally!" Ellen shot her a hard look.

"Enough girls," my mother said, putting a stop to any further disagreement. My father seemed unaffected by any of it, but said, "And then, Sally, how would you get to school? Would you be up for walking?"

That question didn't sit well with Sally because she didn't say another word.

As we ate our pancakes, my father took a drink of his coffee and announced we would be planting our garden this morning, and that all of us would need to do our share. *The dreaded garden,* I thought.

At the sound of my father's words we knew that the rest of our summer would be spent tending the garden before any recreation was enjoyed.

But after breakfast, as routinely as my father expected, we began the annual chore we all hated.

By noon we had completed planting the expansive ground with a large variety of vegetables. My father's hobby produced an over-abundance, more than we could ever eat. We never could understand why we had such a big plot for vegetables. To us it was a huge chore. But as soon as we finished, we were free to play.

Our grey, two story house was situated on the outer edge of Springville, Minnesota. We had a lot of land to roam. There were just a few other houses on the block. At the back of our property were brush and old oaks, and to the south were open fields of alfalfa. Sally and I often went on adventures around our two acres of land. We had a single wooden swing hanging from a huge cottonwood, where the ground took a dip underneath, showing years of wear.

I was eating a Popsicle while slowly swinging back and forth, my feet dragging across the worn-out dip. "Want me to push you?" Sally's voice rang out as she jumped off the concrete step with her own Popsicle. A reward for all of our hard work.

"No, I just want to sit here," I said. I wanted to be alone as I often did.

"That's no fun, Anna. We should ride our bikes to the park."

I decided to agree, like usual, and off we went on our bikes. The only rule was to be home in time for dinner at five o'clock. We raced each other to Sunrise Park, just down the street from our house. On this quiet Saturday afternoon there was not another kid in sight. We played on the equipment for a short time before losing interest. With little to do, Sally said, "Let's go home, this is boring."

As we cruised into the driveway, I noticed a familiar truck. My father was working in the garage as he often did when he was home. In the short time we had been at the park, Leroy Miller had come to see my father. He was a thin and worn-out man with a tired face, filled with lines. I felt both interested and afraid of him.

I knew he wasn't my father's friend, but it wasn't unusual for all kinds of folks to stop by our house. I was used to it. The variety taught me that some folks were nicer than others.

Mr. Leroy had been to our house before. He looked less fortunate than most. He drove an old, rusted out truck that was pale from the sun. I figured he didn't have a garage to cover it. By contrast, we had a garage that could hold two cars.

Mr. Leroy looked dirty. He was wearing ragged clothing and his face was dark from the sun, unlike the truck he drove. I had no idea who he really was, just that he'd come to our house before and that my father didn't really like him.

"I was wondering if I could ask a favor," Mr. Leroy said.

"What's that, Miller?" My father asked.

I didn't know why my father called him by his last name, but sometimes the boys at school did that, too. I pushed down my dismay at his tone, and reminded myself that I would need to call him Mr. Miller if I ever spoke to him, which I hoped I would never have to do.

"I was over at the Schubert farm and I'm looking to buy a tractor." Mr. Leroy Miller's voice was slow and careful. He continued, "August has gone and bought himself a new one, and I'm considering his old one. I'm a hundred short, is all."

I stood there next to Sally, who looked at him with bright eyes. It was hard to know what she found so fascinating about people. I mostly wanted to run away but I, too, was curious about the conversation between my father and Mr. Leroy.

"And I'm supposed to help how?" My father asked with a sting in his voice. I was hopeful we wouldn't see the 'wrath of daddy' that sometimes would rise up from a hidden or unknown place. I was only ten years old, but I was good at seeing things that weren't there.

"Well, Ivan, I felt I could ask you for a loan, seeing how you have all this." Mr. Leroy waved his arm out wide while his voice grew large. That's when I noticed his bloody hand come down on Sally's blond curls.

Intense fear grabbed hold of me and I ran into the house, past my mother, up the stairs and into my room, slamming the door. I felt a catch in my breath as I went into my special place, the closet. One side of the walk-in had a slope over the stairs.

I pushed the clothes to the side and sat on the slant. In the center of the ceiling was a single lightbulb with a pull chain. A chain that my father had long ago extended for us so we could reach it. But now I chose the darkness and brushed by the chain. My closet was the one place that was quiet and seemed to protect me from the outside world. It wasn't likely that anyone would look for me there and so I kept my most special and favorite things hidden in the closet.

As I sat there catching my breath and trying to shut out the thought of Mr. Leroy's bloody hand, I pushed my eyes tight together.

As I felt my heart slowing down, I remembered Sally. I crawled out past the hanging clothes, opened the closet door where I was immediately warmed with sunlight. I crept to the window that overlooked the driveway. Mr. Leroy still stood there with his mouth moving and shaping words, and my father was doing the same. But Sally was no longer there.

The man in our driveway was unsightly and scary, with a bloody hand that he had put on my sister's head. I had to find out what happened to her. I quietly slipped down the stairs, avoiding the step that moaned under weight. I placed my ear to the wall to listen for voices. I heard Sally moaning and my mother's soothing voice.

"There, now," my mother said. "Mr. Miller just tousled your hair and probably didn't realize he had cut himself. We'll wash your hair and everything will be fine."

I carefully opened the door and came out from the stairway, looked out of the window directly to my right, but saw nothing. Mr. Leroy's washed-out truck was gone. I sat down on the bottom step and I felt some air leave my mouth. Now I understood what my mother meant when she said something was a "sigh of relief".

With Mr. Leroy off our property, I slowly walked into the kitchen where Sally sat with a wet head. Her tears were gone but her face was red and her eyes were puffy. I don't know what caused me to do what I did next, but in my relief, I ran over to Sally and threw my arms around her middle and squeezed her hard.

The edges of my mother's mouth turned up, and I couldn't help but wonder how she could be so calm when Sally had been so upset.

~ *Chapter 3* ~

Every Saturday evening, we needed to take a bath and wash our hair. Since Sally already had her hair washed, she only needed a bath. I had to do both, which I found a bother. I'd rather spend my time outside getting dirty than inside getting clean.

"I hate having my hair washed, and water gets in my ears," I protested. "And it tickles."

This never changed my mother's mind about polishing up our appearance. Unlike Ellen or Sally, my hair was light brown and very straight. I had my father's looks for the most part. He was tall, lean and muscular. His skin was very brown in the summer months, and we shared the same hair color. I wasn't so much tall but I was lean. My older sisters had my mother's beautiful hair and skin. I always felt a bit different.

"Anna, why do you always complain about baths?" Sally needed to know. "It's not that bad and you really do need to wash that stringy hair once in a while. Besides, I will use the curling iron to make it really beautiful."

Tonight, Ellen was going on a date with Greg. He was tall with dark hair and dimples. I thought he was dreamy in a movie star sort of way. I knew Sally thought so too. Every time Greg came to our house to pick up Ellen, Sally and I would giggle as they walked to the car where he'd open the door for her. Ellen would gracefully and slowly slip into the front seat, then smooth down her dress. We'd watch them drive away and then go up to her bedroom.

Earlier, in the late afternoon, Ellen had been in her room with the door open a crack when I peeked in and noticed her getting ready for her date. Her pretty blond hair was pulled into a high ponytail, tied with a black ribbon. She had put on a yellow, sleeveless A-line dress with black rick-rack running down the front and along the bottom.

My mother had sewn it for her and now, as I watched her every move, Ellen seemed quite pleased with the way she looked. She twirled in front of the mirror, and then twirled back the other way, looking over her shoulder. Impressed with her looks, she picked up a tube of lipstick and gently rubbed it back and forth, followed by a big smack of her lips. Then she smiled brightly. I knew she was happy with the results.

As Ellen came into the living room, where we were watching *The Lawrence Welk Show*, Sally started giggling and teasing her, "You look very mod for your date." Then, with a sing-song voice and batting her eyelashes, Sally continued to tease, "Ellen is in love." Ellen usually ignored her, but with one swift motion, she smacked Sally on the back of her head.

As soon as they backed out of the driveway, Sally and I raced up the stairs to Ellen's bedroom, quickly shutting the door behind us.

"Ok, Anna, sit down," Sally said while she plugged in Ellen's curling iron. "We have to be careful that we put everything back where we found it," Sally stated in a serious tone.

"I don't know if we should do this, Sally," I pleaded, feeling nervous about using Ellen's brand new curling iron. "She would be very mad at us if she saw us right now."

"Anna, you really have got to stop worrying about everything." We won't ruin anything and besides, your hair could use a style."

While the curling iron was heating up, we carefully pulled out Ellen's makeup. "Ok, do you want me to put blush on you, or just eye shadow?" Sally was rummaging through Ellen's assortment of makeup to see if any new items had been added.

"I would have to wash my face again and I just had a bath," I reminded her. "How about I put blush and eye shadow on you, and you do my hair?"

So I set about picking up the blush and brushing it onto Sally's cheeks in a grand sweeping motion as I had watched Ellen do. It didn't look right. I could tell Sally thought so, too.

"Anna! I look like a clown," Sally responded in disappointment. "You don't need to use that much!"

She stood up with a huff and went into the small bathroom that separated our bedrooms, to wash her face. She came back into Ellen's room rubbing her face with a washcloth motioning me to sit in front of the mirror, and said, "Ok, let's do something with that godawful hair of yours."

As Sally picked up the curling iron, we noticed that there was a small burn mark on the vanity. Sally quickly unplugged it and gasped, "Oh no, I accidentally laid it on its side." She sighed, assessing the damage. "I didn't know it would burn the wood!"

"Look what you did, Ellen is going to kill us!" I frantically screamed at Sally. "What do we do now? She is going to know we did this."

"Dammit Anna, stop it. I need to think!" Sally was now examining the burn mark. "Look, it isn't really that big." I could tell she was thinking deeply about a remedy, when all of sudden she sounded cheerful, "We could try shoe polish!" This idea immediately smoothed over my worry. "That works for covering up scuffs, why can't it work on this?" As I looked at the vanity, it seemed to be very similar in color to my father's dark brown shoes.

"Ok, but the shoe polish is in Mom and Dad's closet," I pointed out. "And, you swore at me."

"No, it isn't," Sally corrected me. "And you made me swear!" She was quick to blame it on me. Swearing was something we both did sometimes; Ellen, too, for that matter, and we knew we'd be in big trouble if my parents ever heard it.

"I saw Dad put it in the linen closet in the downstairs bathroom." Sally said, scrunching up her face as if this was a difficult recollection. We smiled at each other, feeling as though we had really hatched some grand plan. It was as though we read each other's thoughts because only one of us would go and retrieve the shoe polish as not to cause suspicion for our parents.

I had to hand it to Sally, she really did have some of the best ideas, along with some of the worst.

It turned out that I was the one who had to find the shoe polish and not look like I was up to something. Sally always felt my parents thought of me as a perfect angel, though she loved to point out I was far from it.

Coming back into Ellen's room, I had the brown shoe polish in the pocket of my bathrobe. I pulled it out, handed it to her and asked, "Do you know what to do with this? There is a special way Dad puts it on his shoes. I watched him one time."

"How dumb do you think I am?" Sally questioned me and turned the top of the container. "You just smear it on until it covers up the damage."

"But you better read the instructions," I warned. "I think you need a cloth." And, at the same time, we both looked at the washcloth that Sally had just used on her face.

The two of us read over the instructions and applied the brown shoe polish, let it sit, and then shined it with the washcloth. Being proud of the way it looked, we threw the washcloth in the garbage so my mother wouldn't see the stains.

~ *Chapter 4* ~

E ach week, the Sunday morning routine was nearly identical. We needed to be dressed, in nice shoes and our hair brushed so we could be on our way to church for the nine o'clock service. Now that it was almost summer, we were done with Sunday School.

Today I had quickly put on a dress without a lot of thought, only to be reminded by Sally that I couldn't go to church the way I was dressed.

"Anna, you wore that dress last week," she grumbled at me, and I rolled my eyes. "I've told you before that you cannot wear the same dress two weeks in a row. What's the matter with you?"

She pulled out the same gingham plaid dress that she was wearing, but in my size. My mother had sewn them for us and it wasn't unusual for her to make two of a kind. One to fit me and one to fit Sally. I loved my mother's handiwork, but I hated matching outfits and found it embarrassing. Sally, however, seemed to like it.

"Here, wear this one," she insisted, pushing it at me.

I didn't oppose her as it wasn't worth the effort. I took off the flowered dress and put on the gingham one as I was expected to do, and we were ready for church.

We piled into the family car, the Ford Galaxie. My parents had purchased it in 1966 and it was kept in pristine condition. Every week, my father would take the greatest care in washing and polishing it. He wasn't satisfied until that green car shined like an emerald.

There were many Sundays that my father would not go to church with us. Today was one of those. It was anybody's guess what determined when or why he would attend with us. My mother would make the familiar drive to church, and park in the same exact spot; right in front of the second house from the corner of Oak and Fourth Streets, which was kitty-corner from Salvation Lutheran Church.

From our car, we would jay-walk to the entrance and once inside our voices needed to be off.

"Girls," my mother would say sweetly, "you are to be quiet for the entire time we are in church."

My mother would say hello to the ushers, take the bulletin and we'd make our way halfway up the center where we would sit on the right-hand side. This routine never changed. We'd file into the pew with Ellen leading the way, Sally and me sandwiched in the middle, with my mother on the end. On the occasion my father was along, he would sit on the end.

Our minister, Pastor Prewitt, was one to go on and on, and I didn't always understand what he was getting at, but nothing was required of me except to sit quietly and behave nicely.

Sally would sometimes have difficulty sitting quietly, or she'd grow restless. Because of that, every once in a while my mother or Ellen would pinch her leg to remind her of the rules. It struck me as odd, but I actually thought she liked getting her leg pinched.

Today I was listening because Pastor Prewitt said he had a special announcement, that Vacation Bible School would be starting the middle of June.

"Parents and kids," he went on in his deep voice, "it is important to get signed up sooner rather than later." I looked up at my mother who smiled with assurance that said not to worry, we'd sign up right after church was over.

I loved VBS. For one week we would do art projects, have recess and be excused from the garden chores.

I knew that Sally was probably going to protest, saying that she is getting too old, but I also knew that my mother would want her with me for the week. There seemed to be some expectation that my older sisters were supposed to look out for me.

After the announcement about VBS, I happened to look over at the pew across from us, where Danny Parker sat with his family. He must not have liked it because he stuck his tongue out at me. I instantly sat back against the hard pew so he couldn't see me.

Danny was a chubby kid with a round face that always seemed flushed, like he had just been running in the summer heat. And

sprinkled across his nose were freckles.
He was in my fourth grade class at Oakwood Elementary. I usually avoided him, but I also found him interesting to watch. At school, I'd watch him out of the corner of my eye. He had strange habits like gripping his pencil so hard that the lead would snap off. And, at the same time he did that, his tongue would rotate around and around his mouth, like the hands on a clock. Because of this, he had red, chapped skin all around his lips. I didn't understand why he had such an odd affliction. But it was a good reminder to keep my tongue in my mouth.

~ *Chapter 5* ~

Because Monday had been Memorial Day, we didn't have school, but now it was Tuesday morning and we were about to head there for our final few days. We were all in fairly good spirits as we'd be on summer vacation by the end of the week. Because of that, I didn't even object when Sally announced that she had dibs on front seat. She said it every day so I was used to it.

She was in an extra bubbly mood. I figured she was happy about ending her last week, and years, at Oakwood Elementary. By the end of summer, she would go on to seventh grade.

Springville High School was a large three-story, brick building that was connected to a newer two-story building where the junior high kids had classes. Things were going to be different as Ellen and Sally would go on to the same location for school, while I remained in elementary school by myself.

"Anna, how do you feel about being alone next year?" Sally looked back over the front seat at me.

"I don't really care," I responded while I continued to look out the window, already feeling a little left behind. But I didn't want to admit it to Sally

"Yes you do! You now have two grown up, big sisters. It can't be any fun being the youngest."

"Sally, leave her alone!" Ellen's voice interrupted her. "You just look for confrontation."

"Ellen, don't be rude, I wasn't even talking to you." Sally turned back around to face the front.

"Yep, see what I mean?" Ellen said, shaking her head. "I should just make you walk and let Anna sit up front. At least she doesn't give me any grief."

I quietly sat in the back, realizing I was picking at the small rip in the seat. It was something I did to calm my nerves. I often didn't know I was doing it. The conversations, and arguments, between my sisters frequently caused me to dig my finger into the hole, now getting a little bigger.

For whatever reason, Sally didn't say anything more. We were two blocks from being dropped off when Ellen slowed down the Falcon.

"Well, you want to get out and walk?" Ellen stared at Sally. Before Sally had a chance to answer, Ellen grinned and stepped on the gas. I knew this was going to be the first thing Sally would be eager to share with my mother when we got home.

After our long day at school, Sally and I met each other in the parking lot to wait for Ellen, who usually was right there waiting for us. But today, she wasn't. Sally and I stood there waiting about ten minutes past the bell when I was starting to feel worried, as well as forgotten. Sally was downright mad. Most of the other students were long gone.

"I'm going to walk home. Come on, Anna." Sally insisted we get home. I knew she intended to tattle on Ellen.

"I think we should wait, I'm sure she is coming." I tried to sound reassuring.

"We have been waiting here too long. She isn't coming for us. You saw how she was going to make me walk this morning." Sally kicked some rocks, her voice sounding aggravated. "She's up to something, thinking she is so grown up, and in charge." Sally threw her arms out in frustration, and then let them fall to her sides.

I was getting anxious listening to her rant, and watching her exaggerated body movements. "I don't know, we should wait," I repeated again, to no avail, as Sally started walking very fast, leaving me standing.

"Wait up," I cried, running after Sally. "I want to wait for Ellen. I know she didn't forget us."

"Anna, you wear me out," she abruptly stopped, taking a deep breath and faced me. "Just stay here, then. I don't care." She spun around and continued walking.

I was torn as what to do. I knew Ellen had some reason for being late, yet I knew I should follow Sally, or be left to walk home all alone. The walk was a mile and a half. We had done it before, but we had to go around the edge of town, per my mother's instructions. It made for a longer walk, plus we had to climb a steep hill before we would reach our house. I didn't really want to do it.

Springville, Minnesota was situated in the southern and western part of the state. It was mostly a rural and farming community. The downtown area was small, yet bustling. Through town was a busy highway running north and south.

"A person can go a long way on Highway 21," my father had said more than once. His job was located north on the highway, just outside the main part of town.

There were three bridges that had been built over the Des Moines river during the forties. We would have to cross the one that was on the northern edge of town instead of the other bridge that was near the downtown area. My mother thought it was safer to walk around the outer edge of town.

Today was a day to walk whether we wanted to or not. The crossing guard was already gone as it was getting late. We would be on our own to get across the busy highway.

As we stood at the intersection, waiting for the chance to rush across, I felt it was the right moment to take off. Before I could make a run for it, Sally's arm quickly stretched out in front of me, and landed hard in my chest.

I instantly bent over coughing, and gasping to breathe. I didn't understand why Sally wanted to hurt me. Just as I was trying to figure out her intentions, a semi-trailer truck passed by, throwing a warm, heavy breeze on both of us.

"Oh my gosh, Anna!" Sally was frantic. "What in the world were you thinking? You could have gotten yourself killed." I wasn't sure I was supposed to answer the question.

"I didn't see it," I assured her. "I thought it was a good time to cross."

"This is exactly why you should not be alone!" She sounded more angry than concerned. "We are not going to tell anyone about this."

"You need to let me make decisions, understand?" I knew Sally was frustrated with me. I didn't say another word, feeling somewhat relieved, but a little ashamed.

All of a sudden, she grabbed my hand and said with quick authority, "Ok, come on. Run!" On the other side of the highway I stopped to catch my breath and shake out my arm, that had been jerked.

"Gee, Sally, you don't have to be so rough," I said, feeling defeated. I still felt a sting in my chest, and now my arm had been yanked.

We both took a deep breath after the near miss, and took our time approaching the rickety bridge. The structure was old and the foot bridge made squeaky sounds in certain places. It looked like the wood was rotting, and I was sure we would fall through.Having survived a near fatal incident, I felt my heart speeding up again as we started slowly walking over the river. Sally was confident the bridge was safe and told me I should be too, as we hadn't fallen in yet.

Just as we got to the other side of the bridge, and stepped onto the sidewalk, along came the rusty, pale truck. Mr. Leroy was slowing down next to us. My heart was now nearly bouncing out of my chest. I was starting to feel like I was getting sick.

Mr. Leroy rolled down his window as he stopped next to the sidewalk where we stood. "You girls need a ride?" He smiled as he asked. I noticed he was missing a couple of teeth.

"No, we don't," Sally said with a firm and bold voice. "Our parents expect us to walk today."

"Well, suit yourselves," he said in a nice voice. I wasn't sure I should trust him. He took a final look at us, grinning as he drove off.

We stood there for a brief moment when Sally said, "Let's see where he is going."

"Why?" my voice was shaking. "I'm afraid of him, Sally. I just want to go home."

"I want to know where he lives! He says he needs a tractor and doesn't have a farm." She reminded me. "Don't you think that is weird?" She stood there watching the rusty truck slowly drive along Park Avenue, past Webster Park, and then turn left onto River Road.

"I don't care. I want to go home." I pushed away tears as I started walking. After Sally had caught up to me, a familiar car quickly pulled up along side of us.

"Get in this car right now!" Ellen was angry and yelling out the passenger window. "What are you two doing? I have been looking all over town for you," she shouted at us. "The three of us are going to be in big trouble. We should have been home thirty minutes ago!"

With relief, I slid into the back seat, certain this day couldn't get any worse. Sally and Ellen were in the front seat talking in loud, rapid voices. I didn't hear a word they said as I tuned them out. We weren't even home yet and all I could think about was the comfort of my closet, and the "wrath of daddy". It caused my heart to thump faster.

~ *Chapter 6* ~

Ellen pulled the Falcon into the driveway and parked in the usual spot. Not one of us was in a hurry to get out. I was often the first one to jump out, run in the house and up to our bedroom. My favorite part of the day was to get changed into comfortable clothes and go outside to enjoy the fresh air. I loved my time to play before being called in for supper. I knew that was not going to happen today.

"Where in the hell have the three of you been?" My father was quickly approaching us on the sidewalk leading from the driveway to the house. "You were supposed to be home thirty minutes ago, and your mother and I have been worried sick." His face was firm, and his voice was sharp.

Sally was the first to step up and speak. "Ellen didn't pick us up and we had to walk."

"I had to stay after school to talk to my teacher about my final paper." Ellen was defensive. "I didn't know it would take as long as it did. But still, I went to the elementary school only fifteen minutes late and the girls were not there."

My father was scratching his brow in frustration, or in relief. I wasn't sure. His face softened a bit, but he was still angry.

"Get the hell in the house so we can sort this out. You can bet that the three of you will not have an enjoyable evening, and you all are grounded for the time-being."

I slipped around the three of them and quickly ran up the stairs to our bedroom. I changed my clothes and went into the closet, where I sat clutching my doll. I was so relieved to be home, where I could calmly breathe again, however, I wouldn't be going outside to play, and that was punishment enough.

Dinner that evening was anything but happy, but then my father had promised the evening would not be enjoyable. The dreaded conversation sure enough happened during our meal.

"Ellen, why don't you start by explaining why you left two little girls alone, when you know what your responsibilities are." My father was looking straight at her. "Regardless of what you needed to do or felt you should do, all three of you are in the wrong."

I could tell that my father was going to be right about this situation no matter what explanation any of us had. The bottom line was that each and every day we were instructed to come straight home from school. That was the rule, and my father wasn't one to make exceptions. Even so, I didn't like him at the moment.

Ellen was slow to speak, but stuck with her story that she needed to see her history teacher about her final paper, which was due on Thursday. "I only have one more day to work on my report for a final grade, and I had questions for my teacher."

I could tell Ellen was being honest. I looked at her as being a good student, and not one to purposely cause issues for my parents. Sally, however, could not remain quiet, and burst into her blaming voice.

"I had to take responsibility for getting Anna home safely because Ellen left us alone. I'm sure her teacher's name is Greg!"

My mother now chimed in. "Sally, let's not be quick to blame either of your sisters for this situation."

"Well, just this morning Ellen was going to make me get out of the car and walk just because she hates me." Sally was getting worked up. "For no reason at all, she told me to get out and walk."

I sat there thinking that this whole conversation was beginning to sound silly. Sally loved to make a big deal about everything, and it was exhausting. I'm sure Ellen thought so too.

"Sally, would you just stop it." Ellen jumped into the conversation. Looking at my parents, she continued, "She was provoking Anna, and I just insisted that she leave her alone when she called me rude."

"Okay, girls, stop this right now." My father was getting upset again. "It doesn't excuse being late. I understand that there may have been a misunderstanding. However, Ellen you are responsible for picking up Anna and Sally. And, Sally, you are responsible to stay put, and look after Anna while you wait. Is all of that clear?" No one answered him.

I sat there pushing food around on my plate. I wasn't hungry. I couldn't help thinking that I am ten years old and not someone who needs looking after. A lot of this could have been avoided if Sally hadn't had the stupid idea to walk.

"I still think that. . . "

"Sally, enough now," my father interrupted her.

"Here's what I think." My father's voice was harsh. "Ellen, your mother will drive all of you the next two days as you will not have use of the car for school, or work, as all three of you are grounded through Thursday."

He continued, confident with his decision, "You will be taken to and from school by your mother, and not allowed to leave the property until Friday morning. That's when you can have the car once again, Ellen. Tonight the three of you will stay in the house."

I could hear Ellen sigh, though she didn't protest. I got the sense she would like to smack Sally for causing such a scene. Sally actually looked satisfied with the entire outcome as she smiled and finished eating her meal. She really was hard to figure out sometimes.

And then my father added with authority, "Oh, and no dates or friends."

"Oh Ivan!" My mother said, being the only other person at the table, besides me, who was doing more listening than speaking. "You're being far too demanding."

"Hush up, Arlene, and let me deal with this!" There was no changing his mind. "There are consequences for breaking the rules, and today the girls have broken several."

~ *Chapter 7* ~

After dinner, I went to my room and sat on my bed. It was a perfectly lovely evening and I wanted to be outside playing. As I sat there wondering what I could do to pass the time, I couldn't but help think that I was being punished for nothing.

What had I done that was so bad, besides almost getting myself killed? I thought.

That thought caused me to feel angry at Sally. If she could just once not make bad decisions, and blame someone else.

I plopped down on my back, lying there in frustration. Tonight, I didn't want to be with my family, especially Sally or my father. Sally was downstairs, in the living room, watching TV. Ellen probably felt like me as she was in her room, too, with the door closed.

I sat up and looked out my window, which overlooked the driveway and garage. I could see my father moving around. The garage, for him, was like my closet for me. He would go there to be in his own world. It was a place where he kept his special things, the way I had my things in the closet. I suppose we were alike this way, which allowed me to understand him in some small way.

I knew he loved to drink. My mother had said, "Whiskey will kill you." She didn't like it, so my father kept his booze in the garage. He had a cabinet for the whiskey, and a refrigerator for the beer. It made sense that many of his friends would visit him in the garage. I figured that meant Mr. Leroy Miller too. It was common for my father to spend his Saturday evenings in his special place, with a drink, and listening to a baseball game on the radio.

As I sighed deeply, I moved away from the window. I wondered what Ellen was doing in her room. I decided, with Sally enjoying the TV all to herself, I would visit Ellen.

I walked across the hall, and listened through her door. I could hear The Beatles singing *All You Need is Love*. My father had bought a portable record player one year, right after Christmas, when he would get a bonus every year. It was for all of us to enjoy, but it seemed to stay in Ellen's bedroom as she listened to records more than anyone else.

I knocked carefully on the door. No answer. I waited a brief moment before knocking a little bit louder.

"What do you want?" I figured she thought it was Sally as she didn't sound very welcoming.

"It's me, Ellen. Anna." The door slowly opened. "Come on in." As soon as I entered, she swiftly closed the door.

Ellen draped herself over her chenille bedspread, on her stomach, where she continued to look at a *Vogue* magazine. She was smoking a cigarette. Her bed was situated against the wall by the window, which was opened as she blew smoke in its direction.

"You smoke?" I asked, a bit surprised. "Where did you get those?"

"You won't tell, will you?" She was always so nice to me when it was just the two of us. I loved her and I knew she was fond of me, too. Even if she was a lot older, I loved being around her.

"No, I won't tell anyone." I pinched my fingers to my lips, pretending I was locking them with an imaginary key. I kept to my word when it came to Ellen, or my mother. Sally was a different story. I had to admit, Ellen looked so cool, smoking.

"These are from Dad's stash," she confessed.

"Oh." It's all I could offer in response.

"So what do you need, kid?" Ellen looked at me with her bright blue eyes. She had changed into her olive green pedal pushers, and a white, sleeveless blouse.

"I'm bored," I said. "I really want to play outside but, instead, I have to be grounded. I didn't do anything wrong."

"Hmm," she replied, blowing smoke toward the open window. "I guess you are guilty by association."

I stood there looking at her as though she said something in another language.

She sat up and patted her hand on the bed, gesturing for me to sit down. So, I curled up next to her, and she gave my shoulders a little squeeze.

"You are only in trouble because of Sally and her bright ideas."

Ellen still sounded annoyed, even though a few hours had passed since we arrived home to an angry Dad.

"If she had stayed at the school and waited, we wouldn't have been as late in getting home. I could have explained why I was late, and none of us would be grounded."

"I told her we should wait." I added to Ellen's reasoning. "I didn't want to walk and I don't like that dangerous bridge. And we saw Mr. Leroy."

Ellen sighed, shook her head and took another deep puff off her cigarette. "You know, I don't mean to frighten you, but you need to stay away from Mr. Leroy." She was looking me square in the eyes. "He is creepy. What did he want?" She asked.

"Well, I'm afraid of him." I looked down at my hands, realizing I was rubbing my legs. It was something I did when I felt nervous. "He asked us if we wanted a ride home."

"No way!" Ellen lifted my chin to look at her. "Listen to me, you never talk to that man. I've heard that he likes little girls."

A chill brushed my arms and legs, and my chest felt like it was being squeezed. I was afraid to, but I asked anyway, "What do you mean, he likes little girls?" That comment was something I didn't want to think about.

"I don't know exactly," she answered. "Just that I've heard he is known for looking at little girls and offering them rides." Ellen added, "He's a pervert, Anna."

"I don't know what a pervert is. It doesn't sound nice."

"Nope." Ellen snubbed out her cigarette in an ashtray. "It means he probably isn't nice."

Why would my father allow a pervert at our house when he had little girls?

At that moment I thought about Mr. Leroy asking my father for money, and his bloody hand on Sally's head.

According to what Ellen told me, Mr. Leroy was after certain things: Money, booze, and little girls.

Just as this information was starting to settle in my head, there was a loud knock on the door.

"What are you two doing in there?"

Ellen rolled her eyes and told Sally to go away. It did little good as Sally threw the door wide open, and stood in the doorway with her hands on her hips.

"Why does it smell like smoke in here?" She questioned Ellen, who flipped her off. I had seen the boys at school show their middle finger this way, especially Danny Parker, but I was surprised to see Ellen do it.

"Really, Ellen!" Sally looked surprised but sounded amused, too, as she let out a giggle. "Like you need to be in any more trouble than you already are."

"And, you are not invited in to my room, so split." Ellen raised her voice as she stood face-to-face with Sally. "Besides you are the one who caused all the commotion today. The only reason any of us are grounded is because of you, and your lack of good sense."

"I was the only one *with* good sense, the way I see it." Sally's eyes were getting large while she took a deep breath, and made her body taller and straighter. "I needed to get us home safely since clearly you failed to be responsible."

My head was really beginning to hurt. I wasn't sure, but this seemed like the worst day in my entire life.

"Fine, be a little shit, Sally." Ellen continued, "It's what you do best. Now please leave my room."

With all of this arguing, I let out a deep sigh, and I decided the best option for me at this point was to head downstairs for a snack. Since I hadn't had an after school snack, or eaten my supper, I was feeling hungry.

As I stepped into the living room, my mother was sewing. The TV was on, but no one was watching it. My father was still outside, and I could still hear my sisters exchanging harsh words.

"I'm glad you came downstairs," my mother said. "Let's measure you before I sew any further on these shorts."

To be honest, it was a bother for me to let her tug, adjust and pin while I stood there. All I was thinking about was a cookie and a glass of milk when the words left my mouth, "Okay!"

~ *Chapter 8* ~

Later, at bedtime, I had a hard time falling asleep. It was well after dark, and the evening had been less than entertaining, but now Sally was sound asleep. She could fall asleep so quickly and soundly. I swear she never heard anything once she was out.

I lay there thinking about every little detail of the passing day. *How could a day go so wrong*, I wondered.

I took a deep breath and sat up to look out my window. There I saw the moon. Big and bright and round. I gently placed my finger on the screen, and traced around the big, happy shape. Just as I felt a sense of peace, I saw a shadow of a person slip into my father's garage.

Panic gripped my heart, and I rushed over to wake Sally who just moaned and turned over. She was never one to wake up, no matter how much prodding.

"Sally, wake up," I said, as I shook her shoulders. "I saw a person go into the garage."

There was no response from her. She clearly was sleeping and not about to wake up for anything.

I sat down on the edge of my bed to think. Then, I was up, moving slowly to the bedroom door. I opened it, and noticed a yellow glow under Ellen's door. She had to be awake.

I knocked. No answer. "Ellen?" Silence. "You there?" I wasn't suppose to enter her bedroom without being invited, so I didn't.

I decided to go downstairs to see who was outside our house. Carefully moving down the stairs, I hung onto the railing to avoid the squeaky step. The door at the bottom was cracked open, leading to total darkness. Everyone had gone to bed.

As soon as my I put my hand on the doorknob, the door flew open, and I ran right into Ellen.

"What are you doing?" Her voice was low as not to wake anyone up. "You should be in bed sleeping, it's almost eleven o'clock."

"Well, what are you doing?" I whispered.

"Come on," she instructed, and started up the stairs. I followed, both of us avoiding the third step from the bottom.

"Okay, come in here," Ellen directed me into her room and softly closed the door.

"Why are you up at this hour? And downstairs?" She sounded stern, even though she was whispering.

"Well, why are you up, and downstairs?" I asked in return.

"I'm awake because I'm working on my paper, and you haven't answered me as to why you are sneaking around the house."

"I saw someone go into the garage," I said, suddenly remembering why I was up to begin with.

Ellen sighed. I noticed that she was gently holding three cigarettes which she let roll off her fingertips, on to the top of her vanity. I couldn't help notice the repair job Sally and I had made with the shoe polish, which seemed to be only slightly noticeable.

"I was in the garage to get these," she said, pointing at the cigarettes.

"Dad keeps his cigarettes in the garage?" I asked.

"Yes, he keeps all kinds of things in the garage." The corners of Ellen's mouth turned upward, like she was in on a little secret.

I knew about his liquor, and I assumed that storing cigarettes in the garage was also a request from my mother. She didn't drink or smoke. I also figured that she would be upset with Ellen for smoking. Still, I wasn't about to tattle on her.

"Well, does Dad know you are stealing his cigarettes?" I asked, sounding more like a parent than a little sister.

"Look, Anna, I'm old enough to smoke if I want, and Dad has a large enough supply not to notice a few missing cigarettes."

I wasn't sure what to do with that information, but left well enough alone.

"I think you need to get back into bed and go to sleep." Ellen opened her door, and waited for me to me pass. "I've got to finish my homework and get some sleep, too."

"Night, kid." And the door closed me out.

And smoke a cigarette, I thought, as I stood for a moment outside her door.

I crawled into my bed and the next thing I knew, I was startled by the sound of my father's big voice, and the morning light streaming in through my window.

~ *Chapter 9* ~

Friday was the last day of May and the last day of school, plus the punishment was lifted. With all that to celebrate, it seemed as though everyone had plans that evening.

Ellen and Greg were going to the movie with another couple, Sandy Hatfield and her boyfriend, Tom Ganley. All of them had gone to the prom together and Sandy was Ellen's best friend. The two of them would spend hours in Ellen's bedroom, giggling, looking at magazines and trying on clothes. Both were similar in size, and shared outfits, which greatly expanded their wardrobes. Sandy had a dark complexion and dark brown hair that hung below her shoulders. I loved how her hair bounced when she walked.

I had heard Ellen on the phone making her plans with Sandy. We had two telephones in our house. One sat on a cut-out ledge between the kitchen and living room. The other one was on a small table in the hallway outside of our bedrooms. The truth was that Sally and I loved to listen to her conversations. For Sally, it was to gain information to use against her, if needed. For me, I just adored my oldest sister.

Ellen would sit on the floor, her legs stretched out and ankles crossed, twisting the cord around her finger as she talked and laughed. I always knew if she was talking to Greg. She would run her fingers through her hair and bite on her lower lip.

"I have to work tomorrow so I can't spend the night," Ellen said into the receiver. I knew she was talking to Sandy. "Starting next week we can have a sleepover any night of the week. And, finally, I'm not grounded anymore."

Sandy's dad was Dr. Hatfield. Her family lived on Wellington Drive, which curved along the river. Their house was a white, two-story colonial, with a lot of windows and a big yard. Wealth seemed to leak from the homes lined up on Wellington Drive. Doctors, dentists, lawyers, bank presidents, and even the funeral director from Krohn's Mortuary, kept up appearances along the drive.

Ellen would often stay overnight at Sandy's house. I tried to imagine what the inside looked like, and thought my sister was the luckiest girl in the world, right next to Sandy Hatfield!

Sandy's boyfriend, Tom, was the quarterback on the high school football team. He was tall with blond hair. He wasn't as cute as Greg. He had a scar on his chin and when he smiled, the scar seemed to stretch and become bigger. Ellen had pictures on her bulletin board of the four of them going to prom. In the pictures, they all shined with big, bright smiles, but something was strange about Tom Ganley. I just couldn't figure out what it was.

Sally had her own plans. She was going to stay overnight with her friend, Jolene Chadwick. She was thirteen years old and lived at the end of our street, next to Sunrise Park. She was always smiling, as though she were constantly happy. Her thick hair was the color of straw and hung straight to her shoulders.

Jolene lived in a house that had drab siding with some loose shingles on the roof, and the trim needed painting. Her house was what my father described as a run-down shack. I figured it wasn't taken care of because her dad spent more time at the mental hospital than at home, though I didn't know what illness kept Arnold Chadwick a patient at an institution.

I had been inside of Jolene's house one time when we had been at the park. Jolene invited us into her bedroom. The first thing I noticed was that her bed wasn't made and it smelled like pee.

"Why does Jolene pee her bed?" I'd asked Sally later, after we rode our bikes home. "That is gross. Isn't she too old for that?"

"She can't help it, she has some kind of problem."

"Then why don't they change and wash the sheets?" I was stumped at such an issue of uncleanliness. Our lives were very different, and expectations were higher. We all had to have our sheets in the laundry every Saturday morning. No exceptions.

"It's not something you need to worry about." Sally pointed out.

I thought she was a friendly girl, but I had no desire to ever go back inside of that house, or Jolene's bedroom, and now Sally was going to spend the night. I cringed at the thought.

Since I was going to be at home without my sisters around, I could enjoy some time in Ellen's bedroom. No Sally telling me what to do. No doubt my father would be outside, in the garage, and doing whatever he did in there. My mother would most likely be watching TV, sewing, or reading.

The thought of all my family members occupied with other things left me feeling free and happy. I loved all of them, but I loved my time alone almost more. The freedom to think, imagine, dream, and pretend made me the happiest.

At the end of the day, the final school bell sounded and we were out for the summer. Kids were running for the door, all happy and free, full of smiles and shouts of joy. Even the teachers were grinning. I decided it was the best time of the year, next to Christmas.

"Anna, what are you going to do tonight?" Sally was curious.

"Nothing."

"Why don't you ever want to play with friends?"

"I don't know. I guess I don't need to."

The truth was, I just liked being alone. Sally and I were different this way. She loved being around people and having something to do at all times. She seemed to worry that something was wrong with me.

At times I wondered it, too, but I liked thinking and reading more than spending time with people. One of the best things my father ever did was buy the *Encyclopedia Britannica*. This endless source of information was a thrill for me. I loved the smell of the print, running my fingers along the embossed letters on the hard cover, and I loved the glossy pages and pictures. All those books sat beautifully on a shelf, begging to be opened.

When we got home from our last day of school and opened the door, the smell of fresh baking greeted us like a warm hug. My mother had baked peanut butter cookies as a special last day of school treat.

"Girls, you need to change and wash your hands before you have a snack," my mother sounded as sweet as the sugar inside the cookies.

"Can I have two?" I asked.

My mother smiled, showing her pretty teeth and for a minute I thought she looked so much like Ellen.

"Yes, of course, but that's all, so you don't spoil your appetite."

Once dinner was finished and we had cleaned up the dishes, the cookie rations were unlimited, and I was off to play outside with a handful. Sally was in our room packing her overnight items to take to Jolene's, and Ellen was getting ready for her date.

I sat down on the sidewalk by my mother's flowers. She had planted zinnias in her angled garden. Two sides were along the sidewalks leading from the garage and the driveway to the back door. Another side rested along the edge of the driveway.

While I was eating my cookies, I was admiring those cheerful flowers. My mother had planted them only a couple of weeks ago but they were already growing and reaching upward. I noticed the layers of bright yellow and orange petals.

I would have to look up zinnias in the encyclopedia, it occurred to me.

As I was lost in thought, a familiar voice startled me, "Don't just sit there looking at those things, make yourself useful and pull some weeds."

I should have known my father would be in the garage with a beer in his hand.

I took a deep breath and stood up, taking in the number of weeds in the flower bed.

Not too bad, I thought.

I finished my last cookie and started pulling the few weeds that were starting to take hold. With each weed I plucked, I thought that my father had a way of taking the joy out of the moment, the same way he stomped out a cigarette butt.

As soon as I had finished this unexpected solo chore, Tom Ganley pulled up in his old Chevy. He got out, and so did Sandy and Greg. They were here to pick up Ellen for their double date.

"Hello, Mr. Hendricks!" Greg shook my father's free hand.

"Greg, how are you?" My father was flashing his salesman smile.

All this politeness happened every time Greg came to our house.

Sandy smiled brightly. She was dressed in a pale yellow skirt and a white cardigan. Her bouncy hair was pulled back into a ponytail.

Greg turned to me. "Hi, squirt," he beamed, his dimples growing deeper. And then he put his fingers on top of my head and messed up my hair.

Tom said nothing to any of us. He wasn't smiling either. The first thing I always noticed about him was that scar. I wondered why Sandy even liked him. He certainly wasn't fun like Greg.

Breaking my thoughts about Tom was Ellen prancing out the back door wearing a black and white skirt, and her white cardigan sweater, like Sandy's. I figured the two of them had planned this similar outfit. Ellen's ponytail was tied with a black ribbon.

She was met by Greg, who planted a small, tender kiss on her cheek. This moment of sweetness made me feel like I was dreaming, when all of a sudden Sally burst out the back door.

"Hi, guys!" She said in a happy and cheerful way as she came bouncing down the sidewalk toward the driveway.

Everyone said hello to her, except Tom. He looked as though this entire evening was as much trouble as pulling weeds was for me.

After that, the two couples climbed into Tom's Chevy. Before they could back out, my father yelled, "Be home by midnight and not a minute later."

And, to Sally he said, "I want you home by nine o'clock sharp tomorrow so you can help Anna weed and water the garden." I watched my father stomp out a cigarette as he threw out orders to my sisters.

~ *Chapter 10* ~

As soon as everyone departed, I darted up the stairs with the encyclopedia, volume Z. I dropped it on my bed and softly padded across the hall to Ellen's room. I slowly opened the door, entered, and closed it behind me. The sunlight was touching the wall opposite of the bed, making the light yellow paint look like melted butter.

Her room was tidy. The smell of lilacs drifted in the air as I tracked the smell to her dresser. There sat a fresh bouquet from our lilac bushes, neatly arranged in a Ball jar taken from my mother's canning supplies. A warm, gentle feeling came over me like a summer breeze. Her room filled me with joy.

My eyes moved around the room, and I noticed photographs lined up with thumb tacks on the bulletin board. Ellen's friends. Handsome Greg. A junior year of high school, all cataloged in pictures. The first day of school. Homecoming. Christmas. Prom. The pictures displayed a happy story.

The comfort and ease I felt being in Ellen's room made me dream of growing up to be just like her. I opened her closet door and pulled the chain. Light brightened the space. Gently running my hands over the fabric, I lifted the prom dress off the hanger and placed it on the bed. The dress was sleeveless, in a shiny yellow fabric. Then, I remembered the happy moments of my mother sewing this pretty dress and Ellen trying it on in stages until it fit just right.

I let my top and shorts drop to the floor as I gathered up all the fabric to put onto my small frame.

I knew the dress wasn't going to fit me, but I wanted to feel the silky fabric against my skin. The dress was dragging several inches past my feet. I bunched up the extra fabric as I made my way over to the vanity so I could twirl around in front of the mirror. I figured that one day I'd grow into it and wear it to the prom.

I pulled my straight, brown hair into a ponytail, then applied blush and powder. To finish things off, I scrunched up my lips and rubbed bright red lipstick back and forth, in the same way I had watched Ellen do so many times. Then, I smacked my lips like she would.

I dreamed of going to the prom with Teddy Prewitt. He was Pastor Prewitt's younger son. Teddy's hair was the color of a copper penny, just like his mother's. Best of all, he was nice. Even though he was thirteen, I still hoped he would be my boyfriend in high school.

When we were in church, Teddy, his mom and older brother, David, would march right up to the front pew, on the left side. The sun would shine in on them, and that copper hair would light up like a fire. My mother called that hair color "a beautiful shade of auburn".

I took a good look at myself in the mirror. I didn't really look anything like Ellen. The truth was that Sally was the one who most resembled Ellen. I frowned at the thought.

I started wondering what else Ellen kept in her drawers, besides makeup and a curling iron. I opened each one. The top drawer held five cigarettes, a lighter, and an ashtray. I pulled one out, examined it and placed it between my two fingers, pretending to smoke. I wasn't going to light it, just puff on it. I already knew that when I was Ellen's age, I was going to smoke, too. She would have moved out and married Greg by then, and I could have her bedroom for myself.

My dreaming was interrupted as I noticed the lipstick stain on the tip of the cigarette.

Shoot, I can't put it back like that. Thoughts were rumbling around in my head as I didn't want my sister to know that I had been in her things. I figured I would just need to go into the garage, like Ellen did, and take one from my father's drawer. The question was, when? In the meantime, I'd add the stained cigarette to my box of treasures in the closet.

Opening up more dresser drawers, I found nothing else to be very exciting until the bottom one. Inside was a neat collection of items like letters, cards, pens, paper, homecoming pins and a few other things. I lifted out a round container with pills in it, displaying the days of the week.

How cool is this? I thought. I had seen underwear with the days of the week on them, and now pills. I turned the disk over and over, wondering why she had pills.

I bet she takes vitamins, that's why she looks so healthy. I'd have to take vitamins some day, too. I put the pills back where I found them.

At the very bottom of the that pile was a book. I pulled it out. The front had one single word in gold letters: DIARY.

Inside were pages and pages filled with Ellen's handwriting, including the date on each page. I couldn't help the urge to open and read.

May 24, 1968
Dear Diary,

So happy that today is Friday. I need a weekend. Can't wait for my date tonight with Greg. Smiles! I am worried about Sandy. She told me yesterday that she was late. I told her that she should be on The Pill and not have to constantly worry each month. I could take some from Herman's Drugstore for her, too. I honestly think it's a lifesaver! But she said she wasn't sure she and Tom were going to continue going steady. She also said he is mean sometimes. He slapped her recently when they had gotten into a fight. But he was sorry afterwards. I guess I should be even happier that I have such a great guy. I think I may love Greg Doyle! xoxo

I need to make myself gorgeous for my sweetheart.

Ta ta, Diary!

It figured that Tom was mean to Sandy. *Why was she late, and what is The Pill?* I thought about asking Sally when she came home tomorrow, but she would give me a hard time about being in Ellen's room without her, and maybe even tell on me. I thought it was better to keep it to myself.

And, just like that, an idea came out of nowhere. *The encyclopedia!*

I put all of Ellen's things back the way I found them, the way Sally always reminded me to do. I picked up the cigarette and took it to my room, dropping it into my special box in the closet. Before heading downstairs, I went into the little bathroom to scrub the makeup off my face.

With my shorts and top back on, and feeling comfortable, I went down to the bookshelf to find volume P. I placed the book on the step to take upstairs later and would read it when I went to bed. I now had two volumes to read at bedtime.

———————-

Outside, I sat on the swing. I had a lot to think about. I could learn a lot about Ellen by reading her diary. I wasn't sure yet if I wanted to share that with Sally or keep it to myself. For now it would be my secret.

I noticed that my father was in the garage as all the doors were open. This was something he always did when he was working outside. There was a service door on the side of the garage, and one in the back.

I pushed at the ground under me, swaying back and forth when I saw the old rusted truck pull into our driveway. I quickly raced to the back of the garage and sat near the open door so I would be able to listen to their conversation without being seen.

I heard Mr. Leroy's door slam shut with a fierce rattle.

"Hello, Miller," my father shouted to him. "Want a beer?"

"I'd rather start with some whiskey," he said.

I could hear movement and my father pouring a drink.

The men sat in lawn chairs as I heard the legs scraping against the concrete floor.

"I still haven't been able to purchase that tractor."

"Is it still for sale?" My father asked.

"Yes, the last I knew."

"What in creation would you do with a tractor anyway?" My father was already starting to sound bored with the conversation. I had to admit, I was a bit bored myself, but I continued to sit there.

"I have a large property. I work outside a lot, you know that, and a tractor would come in handy."

"Maybe that's a lofty idea, Leroy. You know, given the fact that you don't have the money."

"Well, the 'lofty idea' might be beneficial for me in the long run. I won't beg again. I know how you stick to your guns."

"We are not going to have that chat again, are we?" My father's voice changed and grew higher.

"What, Ivan? The fact that my Ida might be alive if you had a decent bone in your body, and given us a loan for a newer car."

"Damn you, Leroy, that was four years ago. I'm not responsible for Ida's accident."

"Really?" Mr. Leroy's voice now matching my father's.

"Really! The truth is that Ida was drunk. Just because her car broke down in the dead of winter, and she decided to walk on icy roads, doesn't make the accident my fault."

"Ivan, she was driving a piece of shit because you wouldn't give us a loan for a car. So what if she was drunk? She never made it home that night. She fell on the ice, froze to death, in a pool of blood, not seventy yards from our house."

"Look, Leroy, we have had this conversation before. I owe you nothing, just because I work at the Ford dealership. I'm not responsible for your dead wife!" My father shouted in return.

I put my fingers to my mouth, nearly choking and unable to move. Feeling the scratchiness of the garage siding on my bare arms, an image of a frozen, dead woman, in a pool of blood, formed in my head.

Sally's not going to believe this! I thought.

Pulling me back into the moment, I heard glass shatter on the concrete. "Here's your whiskey, you bastard!"

My eyes widened, and I swallowed hard. Pulling myself up, I peeked around the corner. Mr. Leroy was on his way back to his truck, and there was a wet spot on the floor with broken glass spread out like a blanket.

I watched my father get out a broom and sweep up the mess, mumbling to himself. I ran to the house as quickly as I could so he wouldn't know that I had overheard the conversation, and to calm my runaway thoughts.

My evening had been filled with more information than I knew what to do with. I decided on having a snack before heading up to my bedroom. Once upstairs, I dropped onto my bed and cracked open the encyclopedia, looking for *The Pill*.

I didn't know how anyone could open such wonderful books and not get caught up in reading about everything that started with each and every letter of the alphabet. As I scoped through volume P, I didn't find much information about pills that I didn't already know. I grew tired and fell asleep with an open book.

~ *Chapter 11* ~

The next morning I woke up remembering the cigarette from Ellen's dresser drawer. I heard the toilet flush so I knew she was up and getting ready for work. I hoped she hadn't discovered the one that was missing.

Sally would be home at nine o'clock, and knowing that my father had already gone to work — something he sometimes did on Saturday mornings — I ran down to the garage before anyone could notice me.

I found the large stash Ellen had told me about. She wasn't kidding that he had enough not to notice any missing. I grabbed one, shut the drawer, and raced back up to my room, carefully cupping it like Ellen would, and put it under my pillow. Once she left for work, I could put it in her drawer with the others.

I went downstairs and my mother was just coming out of the bathroom. The smell of bacon filled the kitchen.

"Good morning, sweet girl," my mother placed a kiss on my forehead and offered me some bacon and toast.

"Sleep well without Sally?" She asked.

"I guess so." My thoughts were drifting back to Mr. Leroy's dead wife and where he lived. *His wife froze on the road near his house.* I couldn't wait to tell Sally.

Sally showed up before nine o'clock as she had been instructed. Ellen headed out the door as Sally entered. They didn't speak. While Sally sat down for breakfast, I ran upstairs to put the cigarette in Ellen's drawer. Proud of my executed plan, I waited for Sally to finish eating so we could head out to the garden.

Dragging hoses and sprinklers, we noticed the weeds weren't too unbearable as it was still early summer, but my father's instructions were to rotate the sprinklers every twenty minutes. "I don't want to find one weed, and I expect every square inch watered by the time I get home."

Sally would take care of one sprinkler and I'd change the other one, but we had to watch the clock and this was going to be as boring as one of my father's lectures about how our gardens need to be "weed free."

While we were sitting on the grass watching the sprinklers going back and forth, waiting for the timer to tell us to move them, I said to Sally that Mr. Leroy had come to visit our father.

"So, what's the big deal?" She wasn't impressed, as she picked at blades of grass.

"I suppose the grass is getting too long and next Dad will have me mow," she said. Still not interested in what I had to tell her.

"That means I'll have to trim around the foundation of the house." I let out a big sigh, then continued talking.

"You won't believe what happened with Dad and Mr. Leroy."

"Try me," she said, with her fist resting on her chin and her elbow propped on her knee, looking very bored.

"I overheard them talking last night."

"Yeah, so get on with it if it's so juicy." Sally was losing patience with me.

The timer let out a clanging sound before I could 'get on with it'. We turned off the spigots and trotted back to the garden to move the sprinklers far enough to water another area. Then, I ran back to turn the water on again.

Back on the grass, with the timer set for another twenty minutes, I could only think, and dread, that this watering chore was going to take some time. No wonder my father didn't want to do it himself.

"Mr. Leroy's wife is dead!" I blurted out.

Sally perked up and looked at me with huge eyes.

"He said that?"

"Yes. She froze on the road in a pool of blood," I added.

Sally seemed so shocked that words couldn't form. I sat there staring at her, waiting for her to say something.

"Can you believe it?" I couldn't stand the quiet anymore.

"Well, when and why did that happen?" she asked.

"A long time ago, I guess, because she was drunk and Dad wouldn't give them a car loan, which made Mr. Leroy angry."

"What does that have to do with her dying?" Sally looked at me like I had the story mixed up.

"Mr. Leroy said that her car broke down and she had to walk on icy roads. She fell and froze to death. On the same road as he lives."

"That still doesn't make sense about a car loan."

"Well he thinks that Dad killed her because she had to drive a shitty car and it broke down."

"Anna, watch your mouth!"

"Well, that is what he said! She had to walk because Dad wouldn't let them buy a better car. Mr. Leroy called it a piece of shit."

She looked at me with a hint of a smile. "I wish I had been here."

"Yeah, they were yelling at each other!"

"Wow, I can't believe it. How creepy!"

"Dad told him that he wasn't responsible for his dead wife. And then Mr. Leroy threw his glass on the floor and called Dad a bastard."

"Holy cow, Anna! We need to figure out where he lives, and where she died."

"Why?" I asked.

"Well don't you want to see the place where a person died?" She seemed surprised that I hadn't already thought the same thing.

I didn't respond right away as, honestly, I wasn't sure this was one of Sally's best ideas. I was beginning to regret telling her anything.

Just then, my father pulled into the driveway. He got out of the car and as he approached the house, he shouted to us, "Keep up the good work, girls," and then he let the door bang behind him. *Didn't he know my mother hated a banging door?*

We both sighed, hopeful that he would take over the watering and we could finally go about something else, but he didn't and we persisted. Once we were finally done with the garden, he had gotten out the lawn mower, put gas in it, and instructed Sally she would need to cut the grass, and "You, Anna, trim around the house." He wiped sweat from his brow, like he had been working hard, and said, "You may have some lunch first."

Later in the afternoon, my father had checked to make sure all the yard work was all done to his satisfaction and then asked, "Who wants to take a ride to the dump?"

We loved going to the dump. Sometimes there were special treasures there, but we were never allowed to bring anything home.

We responded by screaming, "I do!"

"First I need to collect all the garbage and load it up." This process involved backing the car into the driveway to hook up a small trailer onto the back of the Falcon.

In the meantime, I tossed a ball onto the roof of the garage, a way to play catch by myself. My father had built a wooden box with a hinged door, and placed it behind the garage so that we could keep our yard tidy.

"Be sure to put your toys back into the yard box," he'd said so often we almost never heard the words anymore. I'm sure my father had wanted a boy or two since the box contained baseball gloves, bats, balls, play guns and whatnot. I didn't mind playing with boy toys.

"Okay, girls, I'm ready to go!" My father called to us.

I quickly put the ball back into the box so the wind wouldn't pick it up and take it to some other child who might bounce it off their own roof, or play catch with another kid. I would never get another ball if it floated away because that would be my 'consequence' for not being responsible. I had heard the lecture on consequences and responsibility more than I wanted.

"Coming!" I yelled.

Sally jumped off the steps and we both raced to the Falcon, and climbed into the back seat. Whenever my father drove to the dump, he would drive around the outer edge of town, past Webster Park, turning onto River Road before crossing over the busy highway, and continuing on the gravel road to the big, burning pit that was dug deep into the earth.

As we passed the park, we strained to see if we knew any kids playing there. With disappointment we saw no one we recognized. Driving slowly, we turned left onto River Road, the same road that we had watched Mr. Leroy drive down the day he offered us a ride.

About halfway down the road, I felt Sally's elbow jam into my arm. "Ouch," I said, shooting her a look of irritation. She was pointing her finger out the window on the right side of the car, and there was Mr. Leroy, chopping wood.

"Dad, is that where Mr. Miller lives?" Sally was bold enough to ask, and my mouth dropped open.

"Yes, that's where that good-for-nothing lives."

"Has he always lived there?" She pressed.

"As far as I know."

His house looked as awful as Jolene's, maybe worse. We passed too quickly to take in much more than a run-down house. I assumed we'd come back the same way and notice more.

Our car with the trailer attached, clanked and crunched down the gravel road, throwing dust out behind. It was always the same as we approached, our noses would fill with the smell of smoldering ash, and the rot of other people's garbage. Nonetheless, we thought it was exciting.

At the dump, Sally and I wandered around to see if there was anything fun that someone decided to throw out. I spotted a couple of books in terrible shape, but the rule stood: we were never to bring home other people's junk. It wasn't even worth the asking.

"Sally, Mrs. Miller must have died on River Road," I said as I tossed a rock into the pit.

"I can't believe it was that easy to discover where he lives," she added. "We'll have to figure out how we can spy on him."

She was beginning to frighten me. An adventure to find where Mrs. Miller had died and spying on Mr. Leroy would be quite a distance to travel, and I was pretty sure our parents were not going to allow it. I had to admit, though, I was curious, but this was starting to remind me of one of those scary programs my parents would watch on TV with the lights turned off.

"Mom and Dad will never agree to us riding our bikes that far," I tried to plead with her that this idea was not reasonable.

"We aren't going to ask them, silly."

Feeling my eyes grow larger, I couldn't think of how we were going to accomplish whatever it was that Sally had in her mind.

"Don't worry, I'll do all the thinking...and planning."

Her words were a little terrifying, but often I trusted Sally and her ideas. In a few days time, she would have a clear plan of how we could find out more about Mr. Leroy and his dead wife.

As expected, we drove back home the exact same way we had traveled to the dump. We gawked as we passed Leroy Miller's home. He was not chopping wood anymore. He wasn't anywhere to be seen.

His old truck was parked on a gravel driveway and I noticed he didn't have a garage. Then quickly, we had passed. Sally and I looked at each other at the same time. I was certain we had the same thought, that we should be able to navigate our way when the time was right.

Sally and I never said another word the rest of the day about Ida Miller dying or the conversation between Mr. Leroy and my father.

Saturday evening was the usual drudgery of baths, hair washing and combing out tangles. After all, Sunday would require that my family be all polished up for the reverend and his flock. I figured most of the polishing up was less for the pastor and more for the flock.

~ *Chapter 12* ~

Sunday morning I was dressed in my favorite plaid dress. It was my favorite because it had pockets sewn on the front. Sally didn't like it that we weren't matching. She had outgrown her dress like the one I had on, just enough that she had to wear something else.

It occurred to me that we were getting too old to match anyway. I think my mother was thinking the same thing as she wasn't sewing two of a kind lately.

My father was at the kitchen table drinking coffee and finishing his breakfast. He was dressed in Sunday clothes which said he was going to church with us today.

"We need to leave soon so eat quickly, kid," my father grumbled. I noticed that he was often crabby on the Sundays he went to church with us. I also figured that his attendance in church was more for my mother than himself. But when he was in church, he was full of smiles and shaking hands. It was hard to understand how a grumpy person could turn into a happy one in the blink of an eye.

We sat in our usual pew. The Prewitt family walked up to the front, and Danny Parker and his family always sat in different pews every week like they were trying to find the perfect one.

After the pastor had read the Gospel, we sat down again. My mind began to drift like it always did during sermons. Today I had one of my special rocks in my pocket that was keeping my fingers busy so I didn't get too bored. It was one reason I liked pockets. I felt it was kind of like keeping secrets because no one knew what I had in them.

"I encourage you to ask yourselves in what ways you can glorify God. What burning desire do you have to use your gifts for his kingdom?" Pastor Prewitt sounded like he was yelling at us. "God might be working in you this very moment," he continued. Then his face seemed sad, like he was about to cry but, instead, he lifted his hand high in the air and slammed it down on the pulpit.

"Listen!" He yelled loud enough that I sat up straighter. Even my father's eyes popped open from his sleeping. He was always sleeping during sermons and I figured it was because he didn't sleep well the night before.

"Listen," he repeated, "to what God is saying to you! He has a message for you and only he can confirm in you what you are called to do." I decided listening was better than go to hell, however, I hadn't listened to most of the pastor's message.

"Go out and do good works, but also pray. Pray every day, every minute, every hour!" I looked at my mother's laced fingers resting on her lap, thinking she was praying right this very minute.

As Pastor Prewitt was coming to the end of his message, I felt overwhelmed. I was never going to be able to listen all the time, or pray constantly.

How was I ever going to make it into heaven with all these challenges?

Today I wasn't feeling very good about church. I looked over at Sally but she didn't seem one bit concerned about listening, or praying.

The final hymn was *I Need Thee Every Hour.*

———————

After church, we had pot roast for our Sunday dinner. After we had finished eating, Jolene showed up asking if we could go along to the swimming pool. The pool was a distance that allowed us to ride our bikes.

"You may go swimming after your stomachs have rested so you don't get stomach cramps." That was always my mother's caution about eating and swimming.

Today I felt lucky because I was invited to go along with Sally and Jolene. Sally and I didn't know how to swim but Jolene was such a nice girl that she said she would stay with us in the shallow side.

The man-made pond was an oblong hole in the ground, filled with water. A sandy beach area ran along one edge and curved halfway around the end areas. The pool was divided by ropes into three sections. The first one was the most shallow and where most kids stayed if they were unable to swim. The second and third sections each had deeper water and diving towers. The only way to advance to those sections was to pass a swimming test. I was happy enough to stay in the shallow part as it had a slide and that is all I needed.

As we let our stomachs rest, Jolene came up to our bedroom. I was even allowed to be in our room with them.

Sally and Jolene were looking at Ellen's yearbook, finding cute boys, when something caused me to ask, "What is wrong with your dad, Jolene?" I was grateful I didn't blurt out anything about her peeing the bed.

"Anna, that's not nice!" Sally scolded me for asking.

"It's okay, Sally." Jolene smiled like it was no big deal. "My mom says he has Schizophrenia. I really don't know what that is, but when he doesn't take his medicine he usually goes back to St. Peter." Living in Minnesota, most people knew that the mental institution was in St. Peter, about ninety miles north of Springville.

If I was going to find out anything about her dad's illness, I would have to look it up, if I could remember what she called it, and figure out how to spell it.

I felt I shouldn't say anything more because it was sad to me, but Jolene didn't seem sad. I felt bad that other kids might tease her because of her dad, or for peeing the bed. The thought caused my heart to feel heavy. Maybe I should pray for Jolene because of her bedwetting and her sick Dad. I guess God *was* talking to me, and maybe church today was okay after all.

We decided we should get changed into our swimming suits. I felt strange having Jolene see me naked so I went into the closet to put on my suit. Sally didn't have any issue, whatsoever, and let her clothes drop right there in front of Jolene, who continued looking at the yearbook, pointing out the boys she thought were "really, really cute".

"I'm ready to go!" I said, almost sounding as happy as Sally does in the morning, while I shut the closet door.

We all went outside to our picnic table, on the patio, to wait the final fifteen minutes before we could ride our bikes to the pool when Sally said we needed money for candy from the corner store, which was situated across the road from the swimming pool.

"Jolene, what level are you in swimming?" I asked her when Sally went inside.

"I can go to the tower this year, if I pass my test." Her face and smile brightened with that comment. I noticed her straw-colored hair was tied back in a ponytail, showing the shape of her face. I thought she looked cute this way. "I'm pretty sure I will pass. But, today, I will stay with you guys in the first section."

The tower, as it was called, was the third section that was designed for diving. I admired those kids who could dive and swim like that. They acted like they weren't afraid of anything, certainly not drowning.

"Okay, we can go now!" Sally said, jumping off the step.

"Isn't summer vacation just the best?" Jolene asked, as we rode our bikes out of our driveway.

"Yep," Sally responded. "How long have you taken swimming lessons?" She directed her question to Jolene who stood up to pedal.

"For a while, since I was a little kid, I guess." Jolene was pedaling faster now, making all of us increase our speed.

"I want to be a lifeguard when I'm sixteen," she shouted back to us as she was now in the lead.

"Maybe you can try to teach us to swim today," I yelled to her, winded from trying to catch up.

"Maybe." She pedaled faster.

When we got to the swimming pool, we placed our bikes in the bike rack. The only way to get to the water was through the bath house where a kid, who worked there, took our money. Then, we could continue on through a shower area for the girls. One direction said "Boys" and the other entrance said "Girls".

We darted through the building to the beach area, spread out towels that claimed our spot on the sand. We knew we'd be there for the afternoon.

"Oh my gosh, he is so cute!" Jolene was referring to the boy who took our money. "Sally, do you remember his picture in the year-book?"

"Yeah, he is kinda cute." The look on Sally's face said she wasn't as impressed.

"That's all you can say?" Jolene seemed disappointed that Sally wasn't swooning like junior high girls do. It didn't seem as though Jolene would have any competition from Sally if she were interested in the money-taking boy. I didn't have much to say in the matter because being ten years old meant that no one was looking for my input.

We all had clothing on over the top of our swimming suits, and threw our shorts and tops in heap before running into the water and going under. The best way to get past the cold shock was to jump right in, head first.

The pool always opened the beginning of June and stayed opened through the third week in August, when we'd head back to school. It was the second day in June and we had the whole summer ahead of us. It was the best feeling in the world.

After splashing and going down the slide over and over again, I decided to sit on my towel to rest. Sally continued to play in the water. Jolene had gone inside the building to use the bathroom, and maybe look at the 'really cute boy'.

As I was sitting there, I felt a clump of sand sting my back. I turned around slowly to see Danny Parker standing there. He was wearing swimming trunks that looked like they probably fit fine last year, but now his chubby tummy was hanging over the waistband. His red and chapped skin around his mouth hadn't improved since school let out.

"All by yourself, dopey?" he asked. I didn't answer and wished for him to go away. I wasn't used to be teased, but I was all alone for the moment.

"Cat got your tongue, stupid?" I still didn't answer, trying to push away my urge to cry. I didn't want to be a crybaby in front of a boy, especially Danny.

"I guess you can't talk because you're in the baby section." I continued to look down at the ground in front of me.

"Maybe when you grow up, you can swim with the big kids," he was laughing, but not in a funny way.

Then I heard, "Get a move on and leave her alone!" Jolene was walking quickly towards him.

Danny stopped laughing. It seemed he wasn't used to having someone stand up to him as he had a surprised look on his face. He didn't respond to her, or move, as she had told him to do.

"What are you waiting for, Danny? Split!"

And just like that he turned and ran to where his friends were sitting on towels in the far section of the pool. I felt relief.

"What was that about?" Jolene asked me.

"He's always like that. He likes to pick on kids, especially girls." I replied.

Jolene sighed and sat down beside me and pushed her feet into the sand. I had worried about her getting teased, but now she was offering me friendship and reassurance. I was starting to like her better, and judge her less. It could be God was speaking to me after all, like Pastor Prewitt had said earlier.

"Kids like that have some reason for teasing others," she said. "He must be unhappy about something and takes it out on other kids. Who knows, but don't let him get you down."

Jolene was right. I couldn't let him get to me. He was a kid who liked to show girls his middle finger, stick out his tongue and call people names. The truth was he didn't often pick on me, but I needed to keep ignoring him when he did.

"You ever step on a thistle with bare feet?" Jolene asked me, which I thought was strange.

"Yeah," I replied.

"Well, Danny is kind of like a thistle; full of prickles that sting. You don't always know a thistle is there or how bad it will smart you.

"And, bullies can't always be recognized until their words pierce you."

I still thought it was a little strange, but I guess the words that came out of Danny did sting, not only for me, but for all the kids he teased.

"Just remember that when you step on a thistle, it only stings for a short time." Jolene's voice interrupted my thoughts about Danny being a thistle.

"Danny can't hurt anyone for very long." She added. "Remember that."

I went back to thinking that she maybe had a point, but some stings in life could hurt the heart forever. Instead of telling Jolene that, I decided I should maybe pray for Danny Parker. That he would become a nicer kid. *God is starting to ask too much of me,* I thought.

~ *Chapter 13* ~

On Wednesday morning, only five days into June, Sally and I were eating breakfast while Ellen was ironing and my mother was sewing. The soap opera on TV was suddenly interrupted by a special news report.

I went into the living room just as I heard voices change, indicating that something was wrong. "Just after midnight, Senator Robert Kennedy was shot," the TV reporter announced. "He was making his way through the Ambassador Hotel in Los Angeles when shots were fired. Other people were injured but not seriously."

I sat down to watch, feeling deep in sorrow from the words being spoken. Just two months earlier I had learned the word assassination. Martin Luther King, Jr. had been gunned down at a motel in Memphis, Tennessee. The image of a casket inside a wagon and hitched to horses took shape in my head. My family had watched the funeral on television, which seemed more like a terribly sad movie than something real. I felt a sadness for a person I didn't know because the grief was not only in my house but inside my family.

Bobby Kennedy was described as mortally wounded and though I wasn't sure what that meant, it didn't sound good. My mother and Ellen had stopped what they were doing to watch, and now Sally was there listening as well.

Once again, we were staring at the television with a feeling of shock and surprise. And, just five years earlier President John F. Kennedy had been assassinated while riding in a convertible. I knew how my parents felt about the Kennedys. They were openly strong supporters and it seemed the family was riddled with disaster.

I knew my mother, and Ellen especially, admired Jacqueline Kennedy, and her style of dressing. I could see the influence Jackie had on hundreds of women as she was a beautiful woman, with a flare for fashion.

"The senator was celebrating his presidential primary victory."

The words pulled me from my thoughts. The newscaster had mentioned that Bobby Kennedy was still alive and had been rushed to the hospital.

"All we can do is hope and pray." My mother's voice was so soft I could barely hear her. I was sure we'd have updated news throughout the day and now I was ready to go outside to enjoy a summer day.

I was about to ride my bike to the park when Sally came out and sat on the picnic table, calling after me, "Hey Anna, where are you going?"

"To the park," I yelled in return, wishing to be alone, but now Sally would want to go with me.

"Come here," she instructed me, sounding like she had urgent news to share.

"Why?" I came back, huffing, and let my bike drop to the ground, before sitting down beside her.

"I think this is the week," she whispered.

"For what?" I responded in my normal voice, not understanding the need to whisper.

"To spy on Mr. Leroy!" Sally sounded giddy about her secret plan.

"I'm not sure we should do that, Sally! It's a long way to go and we could get in really *big trouble* if we get caught." I stretched out the words to make a point.

"We aren't going to get caught," Sally said with great confidence. I'm sure she had been thinking about this since the day we drove past Mr. Leroy's house.

My stomach was feeling sicker than it had from watching the news.

"The next time we go to the swimming pool, we are going to ride our bikes down to Webster Park and then we can ride along River Road to see if we can figure out where Mrs. Miller died."

"Are you crazy?" I realized I was talking too loud when she told me to lower my voice.

"We won't find where Mrs. Miller died because we have no idea which direction from his house that she fell down." I was back to whispering now. "It could be anywhere along that road. It was four years ago and there won't be blood there anymore."

I couldn't believe that Sally actually wanted to play detective, like we would sometimes pretend to do.

"Anna, you really can take the fun out of almost anything." She let out a huge sigh of frustration.

I wasn't sure how to respond to her. Pretending to play detective was always fun, but now she was suggesting we be real detectives.

"Ellen said we should stay away from him." I was looking for any excuse to get out of this cooked up adventure that, at one point, I thought was exciting.

"We aren't going to his house, we are just going to spy on him, or play at the park." It was convenient that Mr. Leroy's house was across the road from the river and Webster Park.

I had to admit that park was way more fun, and bigger, than our little neighborhood park. I loved all the different equipment, and Sally's mention of playing there was starting to sell me on the idea.

Every fall my mother would take us to Webster Park where she would gather bags full of walnuts while we played. We were never allowed to go there on our own because it was too far from our house, plus my parents had concerns about the danger of the river along one edge of the park.

It was one special thing I loved to do with my mother. She would take her time collecting nuts and then would sit on the picnic table to watch us. As soon as I had this happy memory, I blurted out, "Okay, when?"

Once the words were out of my mouth Sally would never allow me to take them back. I was regretting ever telling her about the conversation I'd overheard between my father and Mr. Leroy. I had always struggled with choosing between right and wrong. I always preferred the right choice, but Sally seemed to have a way of undoing it.

"Okay, some day when we go to the swimming pool, just us, we will ride our bikes down to Webster Park," Sally was excited, though I wasn't impressed.

"What if someone sees us?" I was back to feeling insecure, though I really wanted to match Sally's enthusiasm. The truth was I could feel the possibility of disaster in doing something wrong, instead of the thrill.

"That probably won't happen!" Sally was really working on me to see things from her point of view.

"Look, Anna, nothing bad is going to happen. We go to the pool like we say we are and then go to the park, spy on Mr. Leroy and we ride home again." She made it sound as easy as a Sunday drive.

Sally had a sparkle in her eye that was hard to resist. I had to admit that she had a sense of fun and adventure about her. She loved being a little bit naughty simply because it was exciting for her. I knew that she didn't have a desire to hurt anyone or intentionally get into trouble. The bottom line, Sally loved taking risks by pushing the boundaries.

I figured she thought if nothing awful happened in the process, she would have gotten away with doing something wrong. She seemed to like that. I couldn't have been more opposite. I had no desire for risks, yet Sally always wanted to include me in her foolish plans.

"What day should we do it?" Sally's question broke through my deep thoughts.

I took in a big breath, blew it out. "I don't know, maybe next week," I answered with dread in my voice.

"Well, I think we should go this week. Remember how glued to the television Mom and Ellen were when Martin Luther King died?

Not understanding why that mattered, I answered, "Yeah," realizing I sounded like I was pouting. I still hadn't gone to the park because of this silly conversation with Sally.

"Now Bobby Kennedy has been shot and they will be so caught up watching that they won't care or pay attention to where we are."

I could see I wasn't going to win any arguments with Sally. She had her mind made up and I was expected to do what she wanted. For my entire life she had been the one to decide what games we would play and for how long. But deep down I was afraid of basically lying about where we were going and why. Webster Park was a longer distance than our parents would allow us to go, yet here we were planning on tricking them. My stomach was starting to bunch up like I hadn't rested it before swimming.

~ *Chapter 14* ~

On Thursday morning we heard on the news that Bobby Kennedy had died. The words stunned all of us, "Senator Robert Francis Kennedy died at 1:44 AM today, June 6, 1968."

Both my mother and Ellen sat there shocked, and sniffling. I felt feelings growing inside me that I didn't totally understand.

After listening to details about Bobby Kennedy having a long surgery and who was with him when he died, I felt Sally nudging me. I knew what she was saying even though she said nothing. This day was starting to feel extremely sad, if not terribly wrong.

I went outside to get fresh air as I was finding it hard to breathe inside my house. The heat and sadness made the space seem smaller than it actually was.

As I figured she would, Sally followed me.

"I want to be alone!" I instantly turned around to face her, knowing exactly what she was thinking. Today was the day we would go swimming, and investigate Mr. Leroy's dead wife.

"Geesh, what are you so upset about?" Sally stood there surprised by my reaction. "Bobby Kennedy?"

I wasn't completely sure what was going on inside my heart or my head, but I knew I didn't feel right about much at the moment.

"You want to go swimming today?" Sally asked, as I expected her to.

"Right now I want to be alone."

"Okay, fine, we won't go until this afternoon anyway!" Sally's voice was calm and reassuring. "I will let Mom know what our plans are and see if it's okay with her, which it probably will be."

I didn't say anything more to Sally. I turned away from her and ran to the far side of the property where trees and overgrown brush lined the barbed wire fence. Sally and I had discovered there were places within the brush that were hollowed out. She had said, "This is like a secret cave."

I crawled inside remembering her words from last summer when we decided we'd tell no one about our secret place. Sunlight sifted through the tangled twigs and I felt like I could spend the entire day there, except I knew Sally would eventually find me.

For now, I could spend the morning all by myself. I was pretty sure that Sally knew she was asking too much of me, and because of that, she would leave me alone for now. It was kind of like a pay off for her.

After I got bored and tired of the scratchy twigs on my bare legs, I left the 'secret cave' and went inside the house for something to eat.

My mother and Ellen were back to watching their stories which I was relieved about because the whole subject of dying was becoming too much. We'd probably see, and hear, more news, and even watch Bobby Kennedy's funeral like we had Martin Luther King's.

I hated sadness, I decided.

After lunch I was ready to let my stomach rest and went up to my bedroom to lie on my bed. Any other day I would not have eaten anything just so I could go swimming.

It was starting to get hot and stuffy in our bedrooms. We had recently gotten fans out from the basement as we didn't have air conditioning. I was sure that the houses along Wellington Drive were cooled off with such a luxury.

Ellen put her fan in her window sometimes, unless she was smoking. Sally insisted we set ours on top of our dresser, situating it just right so that we both could feel the relief. We never put ours in the window because she felt I would get all the cool air and that was "simply not fair," according to Sally. The third fan in the house was moved every day from the living room to the kitchen, to my parents bedroom. It simply was moved to where it was needed most.

Today my stomach wasn't resting too easily and I wasn't as excited to go swimming as I would be any other day. As I lay there, I thought about death and where people go when they die. Pastor Prewitt hadn't really said.

One time I had asked Sally and she told me heaven or hell, depending on how good of a person you were. She liked to let me know when I might be headed to hell if I didn't straighten up. That was usually when we had arguments. The nice thing about summer was that Sally didn't often get into fights with me, or Ellen.

As I was thinking about life and death, Sally came in to our bedroom to put on her swimming suit, and tell me, "Let's get a move on, it's almost one o'clock."

We both changed and I knew we didn't need to be home until at least five o'clock. That would give us time to enjoy swimming for a few hours before going on Sally's little trip to spy on Mr. Leroy.

~ *Chapter 15* ~

After we had put on our swimming suits, we asked my mother for some money and said goodbye, then started pedaling our bicycles to the pool.

"This is going to be such a fun day." Sally rode past me on the road, her blond curls flying behind her. She would always put it in a ponytail once we got to the beach area. I think she just loved the feeling of her hair blowing in the breeze. I preferred mine in a ponytail before I even set out on my bike.

"Do we have to spy on Mr. Leroy?" I asked, still trying to get out of it.

"Yes, there is no backing out now." She continued, "Think of this as our secret adventure." We both increased our pedaling.

The only thing I could think of was how my stomach wasn't feeling rested, and hoped I wouldn't get stomach cramps.

Once we got to the pool and started enjoying the water and seeing kids we knew, I was more relaxed. Sally said we'd stay there until at least four or four thirty before we rode down to the Webster Park. Right now it was still early in the afternoon.

As usual, I saw Danny Parker over in the tower section, but today he wasn't bothering me. I was thankful as I had enough to worry about without him pestering me.

After we had played in the water and gone down the slide at least two hundred times, we rested on our towels. When we had bought candy from the corner store, Sally said we were going to head out.

My stomach started twisting up again and I was pretty sure it wasn't stomach cramps from swimming, but from the thought of where we were going next.

"Do you know how to get there from here?" I asked, as I had no choice but to go along with her now.

As we set out on our bikes, we turned right instead of left, which normally would take us home. A feeling of fear set in when Sally said, "We need to go just a short distance and then turn left onto Station

Street." Sally seemed to know exactly where to go. "It's shorter to go this way instead of all the way down South Street. Webster Park is on the corners of Station Street and River Road."

"How do you know all that?" I was impressed that she knew her directions so well, even if it was a small town. After all, we were headed to an area that was well out of our neighborhood.

"I checked it out." She passed me, taking the lead to show me where to turn.

A sharp intake of air stunned me. I stopped pedaling. "Sally, stop, wait up!" I yelled after her.

She stopped and turned around. "What's your problem?" She screamed at me. I didn't feel any comfort in her words.

"I need to catch my breath," I said.

Sally got off her bike and pushed it back to where I had stopped. "What's the matter with you?" She asked me again without screaming this time.

"What do you mean that you checked out how to get there?" I demanded to know.

Sally sucked in a huge breath of air and blew it out with force. "One day I rode my bike this direction so that I could find the way without wasting any time, and now you're wasting time." She stared at me. I knew she wasn't happy with me.

"You did that without permission?" I asked, raising my voice. I was so shocked she would go out on her own. Still, here we were, taking another risk.

"I did, so what?" She smirked and was starting to get on her bike with the intent to push off.

"Stop!" I protested. "Why do we have to do this today if you already rode to the park to spy on Mr. Leroy?

Sally stopped again to face me. "Look, I only rode my bike over here to find the best direction to go." Her voice was a little calmer, attempting to reassure me. " I didn't play at the park or spy on Mr. Leroy. I saved that part for us to do together."

"Gee thanks," I said. We both started pedaling again, and I felt defeated because no matter what I thought or said, Sally was not going to accept it. She was going to do what she wanted to do.

We continued through a neighborhood near the railroad tracks. It didn't look anything like the Wellington Drive neighborhood. Or my neighborhood, for that matter. I didn't like where we were but Sally assured me this was the fastest way to get to where we were going.

"We need to stay on Station Street until we get to River Road, and then we turn right." I could see she really did know where we were going but even being in this neighborhood would land us in a lot of trouble, whether she thought about it or not. I was doing enough thinking for both of us.

We went downhill just before Webster Park came into sight, giving me some relief. At least now we weren't in some neighborhood that my father would surely think of as run-down. I rode straight into the park, while Sally continued riding along River Road. I decided to let her go on by herself. Halfway down the road, she realized I wasn't with her anymore and turned around.

As I dropped my bike on it's side, I realized I hadn't noticed the shape of the park was almost like a huge triangle. A long side ran along the river. As I looked at the surroundings, Mr. Leroy's house wasn't exactly across the street from the park, but more situated across from the point of where the park and river connected.

"What are you doing?" Sally's voice shook me from my observations.

"Can't we just stay here for a little bit?" I asked, almost pleading.

"We don't have a lot of time before we need to get home." She reminded me.

I really just wanted to get all of this over with and go home so we wouldn't be late, or in trouble. It felt late in the day. Sally started walking toward the far corner of the park. I followed. As we walked together, we didn't say much.

It felt strange to be someplace without permission, plus there was not one other person in sight. I started to feel lonely and out of place.

"Okay, when we get over near the road, we get down on our tummies, like soldiers, so we can watch without being noticed." Sally's words caused me to snap out of my loneliness.

There was a slight upward climb toward the road, like only one side of a ditch. The river was glistening in the late afternoon sun and the sounds of the water were calm. A change of feeling came over me as all of a sudden I thought the river was about the most beautiful sight and sound. One that I hadn't felt or noticed before, but then I hadn't gotten this close before either.

My distraction caused me to lose my train of thought when Sally pulled me down on the grass to get out of sight.

"Anna, you are so much trouble," she whispered to me. "I should have just done this all by myself. You whine, don't listen and are a pain in the ass."

I wish you had done this by yourself, and you're the one who's a pain in the ass. I wished I had the courage to throw those words back at her. Instead, I was here with her because I wasn't strong enough to stand up to her.

I tried to let the anger in me pass. I was peeking over the edge of the grassy area near the road where I could see Mr. Leroy's house. He had so much junk in his yard, like he never went to the dump. There was an old bathtub sitting off to one side. I saw piles of wood and old tires, not to mention a beat up old car that looked like it wasn't being used anymore. *Maybe that was Mrs. Miller's car.* The thought flooded out the sights I took in.

"Sally, do you think that is Mrs. Miller's car that broke down the night she died?" I was starting to feel a little excited at playing detective, but now in real life.

"Well it sure looks like a piece of shit that would break down." She was in a swearing mood today. She tapped her finger on her lips and continued, "I wonder where she fell and died on the road."

"Sally, we can't know that." I was certain we had no way of knowing that. "The road is long enough and it could be anywhere along it. Besides I don't know how far seventy yards is."

"Seventy yards?" She asked.

"That's what Mr. Leroy said to Dad."

"Oh yeah, so it's probably closer to the highway." Sally seemed certain with that information.

"What makes you think that?" I was curious.

"I have no idea," she responded sharply.

Just then we saw Mr. Leroy in his garden.

"Look, there he is!" Sally pointed, sounding a little too happy for me. My stomach felt uneasy and I was now ready to go home.

"Ellen says he's a pervert!" I abruptly said, without thinking first.

Sally started giggling like I had just told her the funniest thing she had ever heard.

"A pervert isn't a funny thing. He likes little girls, Sally."

"For crying out loud. Ellen told you that?"

"Yeah."

"I have no idea why Ellen would say such a dumb thing!" She scrunched up her nose, questioning why we were having this conversation.

"Well look how creepy he is, and Dad doesn't like him, and look where he lives." I was trying to defend Ellen.

"He's not a pervert and I'm pretty sure he doesn't like little girls *that way*." Sally sounded like she had all the answers. I was confused with what to believe.

"What do you know?" I was upset with Sally for suggesting that Ellen would lie to me.

"I'm not afraid of him!" Sally's voice was too high. I peeked across the road and it seemed that Mr. Leroy was looking around for voices.

"Okay, this is kind of stupid and boring." Sally got up and walked closer to the river.

"What are you doing? That is too close." I warned her. Sally looked back at me with a smirk on her face that said she could do whatever she wanted. I cautiously hung back.

"I'm just going to skip stones into the river." Sally edged closer to the river bank, picking up stones here and there. While I watched her throw rocks, I thought it seemed like fun, and so I moved a little closer, but still kept a safe distance.

"Sally, I think you are too close." I warned her again.

"No I'm not. I'm not six years old anymore." Her voice was confident, and defiant.

It was true that I could see her growing up, but she wasn't a teenager yet. However, she was showing ways in which she thought of herself as more grown up than she was. I continued to watch her throw rock after rock.

"Come on, Anna, this is fun!" She shouted back to me, but I still hesitated, torn over doing the right thing.

I stood there deciding whether to join her when all of a sudden she lost her footing and was no longer standing on the river bank. I heard her scream and I rushed to the edge.

Sally was bobbing up and down in the river, her arms swinging around wildly while her head continued to go under.

"Sally!" I screamed so loud that I'm sure my parents could hear me. "Sally!" I repeated. Tremendous fear pulsed throughout my body.

I started to cry as I didn't know what to do. I inched closer and tried to reach my arm toward her to grab onto. I wasn't anywhere near close enough. Panic was taking over my mind and body. I tried to carefully climb down the bank, grabbing onto branches. Anything to get closer. Sally was still bouncing around in the water, but her arms weren't moving like they had been.

As I was trying to move downward and figure out how I was going to pull her out, someone quickly grabbed me. I felt an arm wrapped around my middle, then I was placed at the top of the river bank.

"Stay there," he demanded, and quickly jumped into the river after Sally.

My mind was spinning so fast when I realized who it was. I was desperately hoping Mr. Leroy was trying to save Sally, and not planning on hurting us. The thought brought on uncontrollable tears.

Before I could give any more thought to what was happening, Mr. Leroy swiftly climbed the embankment carrying Sally. He laid her on the ground. He was breathing heavily, as he quickly turned her on her side. Water and vomit came flowing out of Sally's mouth onto the grass.

I clasped my hand to my mouth and tried to get up, but my legs wouldn't work. In my attempt to get away, I stumbled and fell onto my back. I tried forcing my legs to lift me upwards to run, but they felt like rubber.

"It's okay, it's a good thing," Mr. Leroy shouted to me. "She's going to make it."

I had no idea what he meant, but his tone and breathing had slowed as he took a wet handkerchief out of his pocket and wiped Sally's mouth.

Because Mr. Leroy was no longer moving and breathing quickly, I started to feel a little more comfortable, yet I still hoped he wasn't going to hurt us.

He sat there, soaking wet, looking over Sally as she coughed and choked. She was shivering.

Mr. Leroy inhaled a huge amount of air and let it out. "She is going to be fine." He looked at me and told me to stay with her. "I'm going to get a towel and a blanket, don't leave her."

My fear was choking me. I wanted him to hurry as I didn't want Sally to vomit again. I was feeling sick looking at what came out of her. My mother would say her stomach hadn't rested enough.

Oh no, my parents! We are going to be in so much trouble, I thought. I had no idea how we were going to get home and keep this to ourselves. I was wondering how long before Sally could get up and not feel sick, so we could ride our bikes home. I was trying to make my brain think.

"Sally?" I asked, panic in my voice. "Sally, are you okay?"

She coughed some more and I backed up for fear of what might come out of her. She seemed to be breathing more normal, but still coughing. Perhaps she was feeling better, I hoped.

"Sally?" I questioned, as I raised my voice, "Can you ride your bike?"

She rolled onto her back, choked, and was shaking. "I'm so cold," she let out the words as if it was all the energy she had.

How was she going to get on her bike and ride it home?

"Mr Leroy is coming with a blanket," I said calmly, trying to ease her chills and coughing. "Are you going to be able to get home with me?" I asked her with urgency. We really needed to get home. It was getting late. Terrible thoughts were bouncing around in my head. I just knew how upset my father was going to be if he found out. The sooner she could get up and feel better, the sooner we could ride home.

Breaking me from my mixed up thoughts, Mr. Leroy surprised me by parking his old truck on the grass as close to us as he could. As he covered Sally up with the blanket, he told me, "Go get your bike and bring it over here."

I ran as fast as I could and did exactly what he told me, not knowing why. When I returned with my bike, he repeated, "Go get the other one. Hurry up!" While I did that, he lifted my bike into the back of his truck. I raced back with Sally's bike.

"Okay, kid, I'm going to take you home," he said to Sally. "Can you sit up?" She began to slowly sit upright. Mr. Leroy allowed her to sit there for a couple of minutes before asking her if she could walk and get into the truck, because he was going to take us home. I now knew for sure that we were really in *big trouble*.

Sally climbed into the truck with Mr. Leroy's help, and I followed. It was a warm summer day, yet she still was shaking, even with a blanket around her.

Once Mr. Leroy climbed into his truck, he started driving too fast while he headed towards my house. I couldn't imagine what my father was going to say about all this.

~ *Chapter 16* ~

My head was so dizzy that I couldn't think straight. I didn't want to face my father, or my mother, for that matter. I also didn't even know if Sally was okay. She wasn't acting herself and seemed very tired. Her coughing had become less, but she looked sick.

As we pulled into the driveway I noticed all the garage doors were opened. Mr. Leroy stopped the truck, jumped out and came around to let me and Sally out. My father was instantly standing outside the garage wiping his hands on a rag. He was wearing just a white undershirt and grubby pants.

"What in the hell is this, Miller?"

"Before you go yelling and screaming, let me explain how I saved your kid!" Mr. Leroy announced, standing with hands on his hips, attempting to reason.

Sally stood there, weak and shivering, tugging the blanket around her shoulders.

"Why in the world are you soaking wet?" my father yelled at Mr. Leroy, who smoothed a hand over his wet hair.

Just then my mother came running outside, followed by Ellen.

"Oh dear God, where have you girls been? You should have been home long ago. We had Ellen out looking for you."

"They were down by the river," Mr. Leroy chimed in.

"What?" My father's lips pressed together to form a straight line. His eyes grew as dark as a summer storm and his breathing increased. I knew he was very angry.

"Get the hell in the house, both of you. Now!" My father said, pointing a finger in the direction of our house. He didn't seem to care that Sally was as white as a ghost and shivering.

My mother put her arms around both of our shoulders, and led us into the house. "Ellen, honey, will you take them upstairs and see to it that they get changed?" I rushed up the stairs and straight to the window. I watched Mr. Leroy and my father yelling at each other, their arms flying up and down. I watched until Mr. Leroy slammed his truck door, stepping hard on the gas, and he was quickly gone.

I changed out of my swimming suit, into shorts and a t-shirt. Sally was lying on her bed, under the covers, after Ellen had helped her out of her wet clothing.

"Anna, what is going on here, what happened?" Ellen was working on getting the details before my parents had the chance.

I sat on my bed, wondering how much I should say, or what I should say. This wasn't my idea to begin with. This dreadful adventure wasn't something I wanted to have a part in, yet I knew I was in deep trouble.

"We were trying to spy on Mr. Leroy," I said, realizing it sounded every bit as strange as it really was.

Ellen's eyebrows arched upward as her eyes grew large and her mouth dropped open. "Are you serious? There has to be a better answer than that."

I said nothing more as I looked at Sally, wondering, still, if she was okay. "It wasn't really my idea," I responded in truth, because I wasn't overjoyed about the punishment that was waiting for us.

"I didn't want to go, I really didn't." I was pleading to Ellen, like she was going to save me. Or, save us.

"We better go downstairs," she said, "and face the music." Whatever that meant.

Ellen and I started to head downstairs when I noticed that Sally wasn't going anywhere. I went back to her. "Sally, are you okay?" I had to admit that I was very worried.

"I'm fine, just cold and tired." She still had a little cough.

"You want Mom to come up?" I asked, but she just rolled over and curled into her blankets.

Downstairs, my father was standing there waiting for me. His face was red and veins were bulging in his neck. The sleeves of his t-shirt were stretched over the muscles in his arms. I hadn't noticed before how strong he was. I, also, had never seen him so angry.

Before I could make any more observations, or had a chance to say, or do, anything, he grabbed my left arm with his left hand, and spun me around. His grip was strong, and his fingernails were digging into my arm, but that was nothing compared to the hard spanking that came next.

"What in the hell..." *Smack, smack.* The bitter smell of his whiskey breath hit my nostrils as hard as his hand on my backside. "Were you doing...?" *Smack, smack.* "How in God's name could you be so stupid?" *Smack, smack, smack.* "Sally damn near died, for crissakes." *Smack.* "You deserve to have your ass blistered!"

Tears streamed down my face, as my bottom and arm were on fire. My mother's voice shocked me as she shouted and grabbed my father's arm. "Stop it right now, Ivan, just stop it!"

The only thing holding me up was my father's grip. He let go of me, and I dropped to the floor. He quickly turned around, swinging the back of his left hand into my mother's face. She twirled around, and flew into a chair that skidded into the wall, then she landed on the floor with a loud thud.

"Leave them alone!" Ellen jumped in yelling at him. "Get out of here, now, until you calm down. Look what you are doing to your family!" I was afraid for her because my father stood there with his hands balled into tight fists resting at his sides.

Ellen's face was flushed as she fiercely glared at my father. I was certain she was trying to will the monster out of him. And, just that fast, he left, and the screen door slammed behind him.

I could hear my mother's many warnings to us, "Please shut the door quietly." With the house windows open, I could hear the car's ignition, and my father was gone.

Ellen ran over to my mother who seemed so shocked that she wasn't getting up. I was already kneeling near her. "Mom, are you okay?" We both noticed the red splotch on her cheek.

"I'll be fine. We need to check on Sally." Then my mother hugged me. "I'm so sorry. You didn't deserve that." As always, my mother seemed only worried about her children.

The three of us went upstairs where Sally was still resting quietly. My mother nudged her awake to see if she was comfortable.

Looking at Ellen, my mother said, "I think she should see the doctor."

"Mom, your face." Ellen pointed to her red cheek. "And, Anna's welted arm." Ellen was making a point that we might have questions to answer.

"We are going to take her to the hospital," my mother insisted. "Anna, put on longer sleeves and I will touch up my face with makeup."

Chapter 17

We all got into the Falcon. None of us knew where my father was or when he was coming home. I honestly felt that I didn't care if he ever came back. The thought caused me to remember back a couple of years when my mother had reached out to a woman at church whose husband drank too much and beat her up.

Maureen Simmons had two small daughters when she divorced her drunk, abusive husband. My mother had offered to babysit the little girls on a few occasions. All I could think now was that my mother was going to divorce my father because of his drinking and hitting us.

We took Sally into the hospital and my mother explained that she had nearly drowned and was saved by someone who knew how to swim. "She seems like she will be fine, but she is tired and chilled," my mother added.

"I'm going to ask that you go to the waiting room," the nurse suggested to me and Ellen. "It's okay, Mrs. Hendricks, to stay with Sally. Come with me and we'll take her vitals and have the doctor check her over."

Ellen and I waited for what seemed like forever before my mother came out saying, "She needs to spend the night so they can watch her and give her proper care." Worry came over me and I was now scared that Sally might die.

Maybe I did deserve a spanking for not saving Sally, I thought.

The three of us left Sally at the hospital and went home. We tried to eat the overcooked supper that had been ready hours ago. None of us were hungry. My father still wasn't home.

It was only Thursday night, but I asked my mother if I could have a bath and wash my hair. I felt dirty, and wanted to wash away the awful feelings from the day. I stayed in the tub so long my fingers looked like wrinkled raisins.

After I had bathed, I found Ellen and my mother at the kitchen table talking. "Anna, come here and sit with us," my mother said. "Let's have some ice cream."

Besides my mother, ice cream could fix almost anything. "Do you want to talk about what happened today?"

"Not very much." I looked down and swirled my ice cream with the spoon.

"Mr. Miller did a very good deed today," she continued. "He saved Sally's life."

"I thought he was a pervert," I said looking right at Ellen who wasn't quite sure what to do with that comment. I wasn't about to say she was the one who told me that.

My mother let out a little laugh. Even after everything that happened today, she could make light of things. It started out with Bobby Kennedy dying and ended up with Sally in the hospital. I didn't see much to smile, or laugh, about.

"Mr. Miller is a lonely old man who is, shall we say, less fortunate than most." My mother sounded proper and polite. "He served in World War II and, well, he didn't really come back right." I looked at her trying to make sense of what she was telling me. For some reason it caused me to briefly think of Jolene's sick Dad.

My mother placed her hand on top of mine. "He lost his wife and doesn't have much. Never had children, I don't believe." Her words were bouncing around in my head because she was making Mr. Leroy out to be a good person, yet he looked like a creepy man. "I know he looks dirty and not the best dressed, but he really is okay. He doesn't mean any harm to anyone, he's just had a tough life."

Even Ellen looked surprised with this information. "How can you say that?" she interrupted.

"Say what?" my mother countered. "That he doesn't mean any harm? He just did a wonderful thing by saving your sister."

I had to wonder if Ellen thought differently about Mr. Leroy saving Sally.

"Everyone at school says he is a pervert, to stay away from him because he likes little girls." Ellen was talking fast, and looking confused.

My mother's mouth shaped into a big smile and both Ellen and I looked at her, questioning what she found so humorous.

"My dears, you are largely misinformed." She looked at both of us and sighed. "He is nothing more than a loner who lives a simple life. A man changed by the war. That's all. It's unfair to label and judge him as a bad person."

"Why doesn't Dad like him? He makes it seem like he's a pervert and creepy." Ellen argued her case.

"Well, I can't explain your father's thoughts, reasonings and actions." My mother's sincere explanation was beginning to convince me.

"Your dad is most interested in those who have money, who can buy vehicles from him, and those he thinks of as upstanding citizens in the community." My mother looked straight at Ellen who was really processing all of this new information. "I'm afraid your father and I have a different view of people and their intentions."

This chat was reminding me of Pastor Prewitt's instructions to pray constantly. I started thinking that I might need to add Mr. Leroy to my bedtime prayers, because I was feeling sorry for him.

After a long day, some ice cream and a clarifying conversation with my mother, Ellen allowed me to sleep in her room. For as awful as the day had been, I felt special talking and laughing with my oldest sister. I couldn't help but wonder how one's heart could be so full and so empty at the same time.

~ *Chapter 18* ~

The next morning when I got up, my father wasn't home. Perhaps he had already gone to work. I had slept hard. Ellen was up and getting ready for work. My mother was making bacon, eggs and toast. The smell made me even more hungry.

"After breakfast, we are going to the hospital to pick up Sally." My mother kissed the top of my head as she put a plate in front of me.

Ellen came downstairs dressed in a navy skirt and white blouse, with her white cardigan wrapped around her shoulders. She helped herself to some breakfast and already the worries of yesterday were beginning to flow out of the house like a nice summer breeze.

"Ellen, we will drop you off at work because I need the car," my mother stated, pouring a cup of coffee. "What time are you done? We can pick you up."

"I only have to work until one o'clock and then a group of us were thinking about going to the beach."

Just as those words came out of Ellen, she looked up from her food. I was about to take a bite of bacon and stopped. It was plain that any talk about swimming was not up for discussion.

"I'm sorry, I'll change our plans, if you don't feel comfortable with the idea." I knew Ellen was being sensitive about yesterday.

"I think today is not the best day to be near the water. Your dad is very upset about Sally, and still quite angry." I gathered from that comment that he finally did come back home, and I was thankful not to see him. Apparently my parents had worked out their differences.

"He shouldn't be!" Ellen said, as she got up to take her dishes to the sink. "He was wrong to react the way he did!" Her words reminded me of my welted arm and stinging butt. She was right, my father was wrong, and maybe I should pray for him, too. That was going to take some work on my part.

"Well, everyone deserves to be forgiven. Thank God, Sally is all right, and when I called this morning, she was doing well." My mother sounded relieved. "If you are ready, we can get going." I noticed my mother wore extra makeup to cover the small bruise on her cheek.

My mother and I dropped Ellen off at Herman's Drugstore before going to the hospital for Sally. When we got to the information center, the nurse asked us to be seated in the waiting room.

"Is Sally coming home with us today?" I asked with concern because I had expected her to be sitting there waiting for us, with a big smile and the usual happiness in her voice. I was disappointed.

"They sounded positive when I called this morning," my mother answered. We looked up and spotted the doctor walking towards us, without Sally. My mother stood up as he approached, but he extended a hand for her to sit. Concern was settling in my head and heart.

Dr. Hatfield sat down across from my mother. "Well, Sally had a good night and seems to be doing well. She's a lucky child. Had she been submerged any longer, we'd not be having this conversation." My mother gasped. "We monitored her heart and lungs throughout the night and noted a significant improvement from when she arrived."

I noticed that Dr. Hatfield was holding my mother's hand, both of his cupped around hers. He continued, "The water temperature is still quite cool this time of year so her body temp went down, which is not unusual. This type of incident is quite shocking to the system, but with her elevated body temperature and her heart rate normal, she is cleared to go home. The good news is that this could have been fatal had there not been a good servant who rescued her when he did."

"Thank you doctor, and thank God she is fine. Can we see her now and take her home?" My mother sniffled. I was pretty sure the reality of death was gripping both of us in the same way.

"You're welcome, Arlene, I'll have the nurse bring Sally and her discharge papers for you to sign, and you can be on your way."

As he stood and was walking away, he turned around and said, "Just a word of caution, have her take it easy for a couple of days. It's always a good thing to play it safe."

I wish Sally understood the importance of playing it safe. Maybe we wouldn't be in this mess, I thought.

A nurse wearing a bright white dress, white shoes, and a funny little hat on the top her head came walking along with Sally who was grinning ear to ear. I left my mother's side and ran to her. I was so relieved to see that Sally was acting normal again. My mother was right there to give her a big hug and a kiss on top of her head.

My mother let Sally have the front seat for the drive home. "Are you hungry, sweetheart?" my mother asked her as we turned down Park Street to our house. "Anna had bacon, eggs and toast, and you can have some as well, if you'd like." I can't imagine what Sally was thinking and feeling, but she seemed happy to be going home and that's what really mattered.

"I would love breakfast," Sally said, looking out the window as we passed Jolene's house.

I wasn't sure how easy Sally needed to take it so I decided I would take it easy with her. At one o'clock, we all went downtown to pick up Ellen from work.

As she slipped into the front seat, my mother asked, "How was work today?" Ellen sighed, saying she was thankful to be done. Crazy Days, according to her, were crazy. A comment we laughed at.

"Well, how about getting a Coca-Cola at the Sunflower Cafe?" Both Sally and I squealed at the same time.

The Sunflower Cafe was a hot spot in the center of town, on Main Street, and going there was always special. Sandy Hatfield worked at the cafe, and I could only hope she would be there to wait on us.

I could tell that my mother was grateful that Sally was alive and happy. Maybe now we all could resume our normal lives.

"Ah, heck, why not," Ellen replied. "I think Sandy is working until three o'clock."

For as bad as yesterday was, today was shaping up to be much better. *Maybe my mother would let us have French fries, too.* I crossed my fingers.

~ *Chapter 19* ~

After going to the cafe where Sandy waited on us, we went to the grocery store, then back home where my father was sitting in the house. Sometimes he finished work early on Fridays, especially when he needed to work on Saturday mornings.

I had been happy and enjoying my day, until now. It was a beautiful day, but suddenly it felt like a dark cloud was pushing the sun out of the way.

I didn't want to deal with my father.

I assumed my mother had dealt with my father when he came home late last night, but my sisters and I had not. I was sure we were in for a lecture.

I didn't rush in the house like I normally would. There was no reason. I was afraid of him and what he might do to me and Sally, or even Ellen who got so angry at him, that he left in the first place. Sally bravely walked in while Ellen and my mother carried in three bags of groceries from the Red Owl.

My father greeted us at the door, hugging Sally like he really cared. I could not understand how he could be so hateful one day and somewhat loving the next. I squeezed past their embrace and began to remove items from the paper bags sitting on the kitchen table.

"Put those groceries away and then we are going to sit here and talk." My father's gruff voice was intended for all of us.

We all sat around the kitchen table like we would for a meal, but it was the middle of the afternoon. It felt weird to sit there, looking at each other without any food in front of us to keep us busy.

"I do not understand what happened yesterday, or why it happened," my father scoffed, breaking the silence and glancing at all of us. "I know what Leroy told me and that, you, Sally, are lucky to be alive." She rolled her eyes though he didn't seem to notice. "Care to tell me why you were down by the river when you are never allowed to go there by yourselves?"

"Ivan, I think Sally has had enough distress without reliving it.

Anna, too, for that matter." My mother said boldly before either of us could even begin to talk. "I feel the main thing is that a lesson was learned and we should be grateful that the girls are sitting here, alive and healthy."

"Arlene, I fail to see how you can be so lax." He looked at her harshly, but his face softened when he noticed the bruise on her cheek. He quickly turned away from her and hardened his features again.

He took a deep breath and let it out, then pushed his back straight into the chair. "Look, Arlene, girls, this kind of thing cannot be tolerated. Breaking rules and running all over creation without permission does not happen without consequences." He had uttered similar words before.

Here we go again, I thought.

"There will be no swimming for at least a week. For all of you!" I gulped thinking that Ellen wasn't even involved, yet she was paying the price for Sally's disaster. Just then I felt a sting of anger. At Sally. At my father. Why was it that every time Sally had gotten into trouble, the rest of us were punished as well?

Here I was listening to my father go on and on, and I could only think about how I was the one who got walloped on the backside, and my mother was slapped and thrown to the floor.

Sally was spared any physical punishment because she nearly drowned. And now Ellen was not allowed to go to the pool or the beach at Silver Lake, which was outside of town. And here Sally sat looking like she was bored with the whole conversation. Had she really learned a lesson? I wasn't sure.

My father seemed to be looking for some kind of answers or apologies, I wasn't sure, but I was ready to be out of his sight.

"You know, this better sink in, girls, because I will not have another incident like this, you hear?" Not one of us answered, but we all nodded our heads.

He stood up and the chair legs scraped the linoleum as he looked firmly at my mother. "Good God, Arlene, get these kids into swimming lessons, and start watching them as close as you watch those damn soap operas." Then he went out to the garage, taking his hostility with him. The bang of the screen door expressed his irritation as a last word.

My heart shattered.

With my father out of sight, I climbed the stairs to my room, intentionally stepping on the squeaky one, pretending it was him. I went into the closet just to sit.

I wanted the dark.

I wanted the quiet.

I wanted to turn off the world.

~ *Chapter 20* ~

I woke up Saturday morning to see the sun smiling brightly through my window, promising, I hoped, to force out the horrible events of the past couple of days.

Just as I had expected, the only thing on television was the funeral of Robert F. Kennedy, not the usual cartoons. Ellen sat on the sofa with her legs tucked underneath her, eating a bowl of cereal. Sally was still asleep and my mother was sitting in her chair, sipping coffee. And, my father was working.

I sat down on the floor to watch hundreds and thousands of people lined up outside a very large Catholic church in New York City. I had overheard adults say that the Catholics had many children. The Kennedys were proof, and Bobby Kennedy's wife, Ethel, was expecting their eleventh child.

"I don't understand all the hate in the world," my mother said as she wiped her sniffles away. The air had been getting heavy with humidity over several days, and my heart was about as heavy with sadness. "People are still grieving about Martin Luther King, Jr.," she continued, both hands around her coffee cup, about to take another drink.

"This certainly changes things for the upcoming election," Ellen added to the comments. "What a horrible way to die, and for it to happen twice, in one family."

"It's a terrible tragedy, for sure." My mother's voice was soft and calm, though she sounded like she might cry.

We watched the family of Bobby Kennedy enter the church, dressed in black. Mrs. Kennedy had a black net covering her face. Little girls wore something like white handkerchiefs on their heads, and white gloves. Jackie Kennedy also wore black, a contrast from her usual wardrobe. And, Martin Luther King's widow, Coretta King, was also wearing a black dress and a black pillbox hat. Several other important, and well-known people, gathered into church pews as the man on the news mentioned their names.

At our church we had one pastor, but this church had several, wearing odd hats, with various colors of red and blue capes over the top of their white robes. They processed to the front of the church where they sat in 'royal' chairs. The casket holding Bobby Kennedy's body was draped with the American flag, while several men stood near it.

The camera panned over family and guests, showing extremely sad faces, and I noticed my mother couldn't hold on to her tears anymore. They fell slowly and softly down her pretty face, and a lump formed in my throat.

I felt like I couldn't take much more, yet I couldn't make myself not watch either. Dark and sad music filled the enormous church. The priest said some words and then Bobby Kennedy's brother, Senator Edward Kennedy, walked to the front with a folded piece of paper.

He stood at the podium, in front of a microphone, and started to speak, his voice became very shaky. I looked to see both my mother and Ellen softly weeping.

Edward Kennedy said, "As he said many times, in many parts of this nation, to those he touched and who sought to touch him: "'Some men see things as they are and say, 'Why?' I dream of things that never were and say, 'Why not?'"

For some reason this caused me to let go of some tears as well and I wiped them away as fast as they came. By this time, Sally was up, bringing me back to reality.

"What happens now?" Ellen asked.

"America grieves," my mother responded. "Again." I knew she was remembering both John Kennedy, and Martin Luther King, Jr.

We all watched the funeral conclude with the casket being taken out by several men, and later transported by train from New York City to Washington, D.C. The final resting place would be Arlington National Cemetery, where JFK was buried.

"I'm hungry!" Sally broke the heartbreaking silence, as she headed to the kitchen for something to eat. The rest of us felt too numb from the heavy despair to say much of anything.

Sally seemed as though she was back to her normal self, yet she was still supposed to take it easy for a couple of days. I wondered if she would be able to obey that order. She could be so different from the rest of us, except maybe my father. I questioned in my mind how she could seem so unaffected by life's events as either shown on TV, or by her her own near-drowning experience.

Even though the heat and humidity was stifling upstairs, I went up to my room to think. It occurred to me that today would be a perfect day to spend at the swimming pool.

I didn't care what Sally's rules were about the fan, I turned it so it was blowing at me on the high setting. I plopped down on my bed, disappointed I wasn't cooling off in the water, nor would I be for a whole week.

Thanks, Sally!

I couldn't help wondering about death. I wanted to understand it better, but it was so mixed up. All I knew for sure was that it's forever. Maybe the encyclopedia would have answers, but probably not the ones I was looking for.

~ *Chapter 21* ~

Sunday, we went to church. My father chose not to go with us which I was thankful for, because I was avoiding him. Everything was as routine as any other Sunday. However, as soon as I saw Maureen Simmons and her two little girls, I still wasn't sure what was going to happen with my parents, even though it seemed like everything had gone back to normal. I wished that I, too, could forget it so easily.

Pastor Prewitt reminded the congregation, once again, that on Monday, June 17, Vacation Bible School would begin. This, at least, was a happy reminder since life at home still wasn't as pleasant as I'd have liked it.

When the minister started his sermon, I starting thinking about other things like how happy Mrs. Simmons and her daughters must be, after her divorce, without Mr. Simmons in their home. But then I remembered my mother saying Maureen had to get a job, and the girls needed to have a babysitter.

Maybe I didn't really want that for my family after all. I liked having my mother at home, baking, sewing and cooking. If she divorced my father, people would look at us differently. The same way I was looking at Mrs. Simmons right now. Her life was broken.

Next to me, Sally was restlessly swinging her legs back and forth until she accidentally kicked the back of the pew in front of us, rattling my thoughts. The loud thud caused people to look in our direction, and Pastor Prewitt briefly paused with his sermon. My mother nudged Sally's leg and the look on her face said more than words. I knew what she was saying without saying it.

At the end of the service the pastor said special prayers for all kinds of people including Bobby Kennedy's family. He said, "In this life, we will have darkness. We cannot escape from the events of this earthly life, therefore, we need to be heavenly-minded." Pastor Prewitt became quiet for several seconds before he continued, "God has numbered our days, so go out and be good servants, because one day he will call you home. Be prepared."

I wasn't sure about the rest of my family, but Pastor Prewitt often made me feel more afraid than hopeful. Maybe that was why my father stayed away from church as much as possible. The good Lord knew my father, of all people, should be prepared and heavenly-minded. But he wasn't there to hear the message so he didn't need to worry about such things.

Later in the day, I could hear music inside Ellen's room. Sally was outside with Jolene, who had just heard about her "incident," which my family was now calling it instead of almost drowning.

I knocked on Ellen's door and she said, "Come in!" I peeked my head around the door. "Come in, Anna, I already said it was okay." I wasn't sure why I was standing there except I was feeling down for some reason.

"Close the door," she said and got out a cigarette. "Something wrong?"

She was listening to a song with words that caught my attention. "A time to be born, a time to die, a time to plant, a time to reap."

"Anna?" Ellen's voice broke my silence.

"What is that song and why are you listening to it?" I asked.

Then I heard the words, "And a time to every purpose under heaven."

"It's a song by the Byrds," she said. "A song about a bible passage." Ellen lifted the bible from her nightstand and started paging through it. "See," she said, pointing to Ecclesiastes 3:1-8. "Right here, these words have been turned into a song about a time for everything." She continued reading the passage to me.

I hadn't given much consideration to reading the bible, but maybe if I did I would be less afraid of the things Pastor Prewitt often said to us.

"I was listening to this to try and make sense of life," Ellen added. "Or death."

I was curious. "Well does it make you happy or sad?"

"I guess a little of both." We looked at each other, and Ellen squeezed me into her side. "You've had a tough couple of days," she said, changing the subject. "Something you want to talk about?"

"I don't know." It was true, I wasn't sure what was going on inside my heart and head. "Are Mom and Dad getting a divorce?"

"Oh, my! No!" Ellen sat up straighter to face me. "Why do you ask that? Because Dad got so angry?"

"He can be so mean," I said. "He scares me when he gets mad." I let out a small sigh and looked down at my hands.

"Yes, I know, but he does love his family." I could tell she was trying to reassure me.

I didn't really see how she could think that. I glanced over to Ellen's pictures and remembered reading in her diary about Tom Ganley hitting Sandy.

Were all men and boys mean? I thought.

"Love is nice. People don't hit and yell at others if they love them," I said in a small voice, a little worried about saying it, but it was too late.

"You're right and I know it's complicated to understand. Some people have bad tempers, but it doesn't mean they are hateful."

I had to ask, "Do you read that in the bible?"

Ellen giggled. "You are funny. Yes, sometimes I do read that in the bible, or hear it in church." She paused to think, and placed her fingertips on her chin. "And, sometimes, I just know in my heart that some people have words and actions that don't always match their true intentions."

She was right, this was complicated.

"I don't know, honey, sometimes you just have to close your eyes to see things differently."

I sure loved Ellen, but she was really starting to sound like a grown-up.

~ *Chapter 22* ~

A few days had passed and about the only way to stay cool was go outside, or sit in front of the fan. I was sitting on the cool linoleum floor near the fan, playing in my mother's button jar while she was sewing.

Every week the local newspaper was published and my parents would read every page like their life hinged on the information it contained. "It's in our best interest to know what is happening in our community," my father said as he rolled it up and playfully tapped it on someone's head, whomever happened to be closest to him at the time.

Today was different as my father came storming into the house, throwing the paper on the table, saying, "Arlene, come look at this!" He barked like a mad dog. I ran after her, noticing he was firmly pointing to the headline: 'Man Saves Girl From Drowning in River'.

"What the hell is this doing in the paper? On the front page, no less. This is not good for my reputation!"

"Really, Ivan, I don't see how you can think that way!" My mother looked at the paper on the table and continued, "And, it's on the lower half of the front page, not the leading story." Her attempts to minimize it weren't working as my father stood up tall and crossed his arms over his chest.

"I am an upstanding man in this community, and I can't have people thinking that my children are unsupervised brats!"

"Our children are wonderful and don't call them brats," my mother shot back.

I quietly eased back to the button jar, where I was able to see both of my parents through the arch, listening closely to every word.

"Sally and Anna were disobedient, sneaking off, lying, conniving — nearly dying in the process — I don't want people to know that!" He pushed out a huge sigh and placed his hands on his hips. I crossed my fingers, hoping his wrath wasn't going to break loose again. "I want people to think our children are as wonderful as you do, but they need to behave."

"Well it's in the paper now, isn't it?" My mother sounded helpless. "Look at it as a warning for other children to stay away from the peril of the river."

I wished my father didn't see me as such a disobedient brat. I was feeling uncertain. I tried hard to be good, yet it wasn't working. I just wanted him to love me, like Ellen said he did, but I didn't feel it.

"I've the notion to go to Miller's house," my father said, shaking his head in frustration, "and give him a piece of my mind."

"If you do that, take this apple pie to him," my mother said calmly as she pointed to a pie sitting on the counter, "to thank him for being Sally's angel. It's the least we can do."

My father rubbed the palm of his hand along his forehead. "Take the damn pie yourself!" And he stomped out of the house, like a child.

~ *Chapter 23* ~

And, the next day, that is exactly what we did. My mother took me and Sally to Mr. Leroy's house to deliver the pie that sat untouched on our counter, and to say thank you for being the kind of servant our pastor said people should be.

"Girls, I want you to come with me to the door," my mother ordered. "We are going to be polite and offer Mr. Miller this pie. Sally, you will thank him for saving you."

We reluctantly trudged to the door, each of us tagging slightly behind my mother. She rapped on the door. We stood there for a longer period of time than anyone coming to my house would, but we also had several people in our house who could welcome a visitor.

I suddenly remembered there was only one person who lived here. "Maybe he is busy," I said to my mother, hoping that we'd just turn around and go home. I was sure my father wouldn't be pleased that we were standing on Mr. Leroy's doorstep.

"We need to be patient," my mother replied, standing tall, holding the pie with Reynolds Wrap neatly pinched all around the edges.

After a few moments, my mother pounded on the door again, louder this time. It seemed to work because along came Mr. Leroy. He looked like we had just interrupted him from a nap as his hair was a mess, and he looked groggy.

"Arlene?" he asked as he came out of the house to stand on the stoop with us. At our house, we invited people inside. I was relieved his rules were different. "What in the world are you doing here?" he questioned. I looked up at his scruffy face. He needed to shave and I quickly thought about how my father shaved every day.

"Leroy," my mother's voice brought me back to why we were here, "we have a little token of thanks for you. I made you an apple pie." My mother flashed a big smile at him.

"Thanks?" Mr. Leroy was all questions as he didn't seem to know what she was getting at.

"Well, I brought the girls to thank you in person for being there for them last week." My mother nudged Sally with her elbow.

"Oh, that! It's what anyone would do in time of need," he responded. " I heard distress and didn't think twice about it."

Sally perked up and offered, "Thank you, Mr. Miller, for saving my life!"

I was fairly certain she had rehearsed that a few times before saying it with sincerity. I said nothing, and just stood there, thinking that Sally's thanks was enough for both of us.

"Well, here, I know a pie isn't much of a thank you, but I want you to know we are grateful you were there to, you know, um, save Sally from...," my mother cleared her throat, "that awful incident."

"I appreciate that, Arlene, and I will enjoy this." He smiled, genuinely, but I was still bothered by his missing teeth.

"Well, we will be off, and you stay cool now," my mother said, and instructed us to tell Mr. Miller good-bye.

Before we got too far, my mother turned around and said, "I'm sorry to say Ivan wasn't anything too thrilled with the article in the paper." Sally brightened at that comment.

"Well, as you and I both know, the medical staff needs to report a near-drowning to the County. This kind of thing becomes newsworthy in a quick manner. Not much we can do about that."

Mr. Leroy stood there holding his pie and continued, "I think it's information that will hopefully prevent another situation like yours."

"I think so, too," she responded. "Have a fine day."

Once we were back home, Sally raced into the house, sat down at the kitchen table and spread out the newspaper to read what was said about her. She was downright giddy about seeing her name in the paper, and started to read out loud:

Man Saves Girl from Drowning in River
Late on Thursday afternoon, June 6, Sally Hendricks and her sister, Anna, were playing near the Des Moines River when Sally fell in. She was unable to swim and submerged several minutes before a good samaritan, Leroy Miller, who lives across the road, heard cries of

distress.

"I just reacted to the screams and cries," Miller said. "I'm happy the girls are safe, but I'm no hero." Miller said he didn't think twice about quickly jumping in to pull the older girl out of the water.

Sally Hendricks, age 12, spent a night at the hospital, where she was under observation for signs of near-drowning. She was discharged after 24 hours.

Sally is the daughter of Ivan and Arlene Hendricks, Springville.

"I'm so grateful Mr. Miller was an angel that day," Mrs. Hendricks stated by phone. "God is to be praised for providing good servants."'

"I'm going to cut this out and save it," Sally exclaimed, until my mother reminded her that nothing would be cut from the paper until it had been read by everyone and ready to be discarded.

"I don't think Dad wants to read this part anyway," she continued. I had told Sally how upset the headline made our father.

"Well, he has already seen it and he may be interested with what's on the other side," my mother offered a stern reply.

Clearly, Sally was worried the paper would get tossed out before she could save her article. "Well, just don't throw it out," she insisted. Before Sally could win any arguments, my mother assured her the newspaper would be hers as soon as it had been read completely. How she could be so thrilled about the now-called 'incident' was beyond me.

~ *Chapter 24* ~

I t was Friday night and Ellen was staying overnight with Sandy. They had planned a double date with their boyfriends. Sally and I were sitting around outside, in the cool grass, trying to figure out what to do.

"I have an idea," Sally said. "Let's go fix your hair so you can have curls like mine."

"You mean with Ellen's curling iron?" I asked even though I knew what she meant.

"Of course, silly!" She raked her fingers through my hair like she was combing it. "We haven't made your hair beautiful like mine...yet!"

"Okay!" I got up and ran to the house, beating Sally through the door first and up the steps to Ellen's room. She was right on my heels. We giggled as we caught our breath.

"Where is the curling iron?" Sally was confused as she looked around the room. Ellen usually left it sitting out, or stored it in her vanity drawer after it cooled down.

"She used it right before her date and left it in the bathroom sink," I offered as I recalled watching Ellen getting ready. "I'll go get it."

After I retrieved the curling iron, Sally said, "Well, let's have you sit at her vanity where you can watch in the mirror." She patted the seat of the chair for me to sit, and then plugged it in.

"We better not set it on the vanity again," I said, pointing to the polished mark from the last mishap. "It still looks like we really fixed it up good," I added, confirming how clever we had been.

"Oh yeah, good idea, I'll set it on the bed." She smiled, continuing, "While it heats up, we'll brush through your hair."

I was so excited to have curls. To be honest, I was jealous that Sally had curls all the time. No one else in my family had them, and who knew how she had a head full of ringlets.

Sally started brushing a little too hard as she struggled to get the snarls out. "Ouch," I complained, "that hurts."

"Don't you ever brush your hair?" She scowled at me. "You're going to have to put up with it if you want to look pretty." As I sat there and let her pull my hair, tears stung the corners of my eyes, but I didn't object.

She kept at it until it was just right and was able to run a comb through without any snags. When she set the comb down, she spit on her finger and touched the barrel of the curling iron. A small hiss whispered from the heated tool, and she said, "Ouch, it's hot, and ready!"

"Anna, you are lucky that you can choose when you want curls," she said, frowning when she looked at herself in the mirror. "Sometimes I just want straight hair, but not as awful as yours."

I said nothing as she lifted a section of hair and wrapped it around the curling iron, twisting it and holding it in place. "One, two, three, four...." She counted up to ten before she released my hair from the iron. A tight curl sprung loose and she let out a high shrill. "Oh my gosh, look, Anna! A real curl, like mine!" I had to admit I was quite pleased with what I saw.

"I love it, now do the rest!" I urged her to continue. Sally kept curling sections of hair until my entire head was full of curls. I looked in the mirror, turning my head to the right and then to the left before taking a hand mirror to see the back. Some areas were tighter than others which reminded me of the times when my mother would give our neighbor lady, Phyllis Armstrong, a permanent right at our kitchen table. The smell of ammonia would chase all of us out of the house, pinching our noses.

When my mother was done with her, she had such tight little knots that it'd take months for it to loosen up. I thought it looked terrible, but Mrs. Armstrong would go into our bathroom and admire it like she was the most beautiful woman in all of Springville.

After we were done with my hair, Sally pulled the plug on the curling iron and placed it back in the sink in the little bathroom.

"Now what should we do?" I asked.

"I don't know, let's see what new makeup Ellen has," she suggested.

"I don't really want to," I said as I was happy enough to have curly hair.

"I have a secret!" Sally's eyes glistened and she looked over at Ellen's bulletin board. I looked in the same direction, thinking she was going to make me work for her little secret. I had a secret, too, but wasn't about to share because then it wouldn't be a secret anymore.

"Do you want to tell me?" I asked because I knew she had a tough time keeping anything private.

She scrunched up her mouth as if to decide. Instead she threw out hints. "Well, I'm not sure if Jolene would like it shared, so you'd have to promise not to ever tell anyone."

I wasn't sure what to say. I was curious to know but I didn't want to beg. As I sat there quietly waiting for her to decide if I should know, she got up and walked over to Ellen's prom picture on the bulletin board, and placed a finger right on top of Tom Ganley's face.

Sally looked back at me fluttering her eyelashes and I straightened up, wondering what she was trying to say without saying it.

"You like Tom?" The words fell out of my mouth, and I winced like I was in pain.

Her face twisted up and she said, "What's the matter with you? Of course I don't like him *that way!*"

"Then what are you talking about?"

Sally came over to the bed and sat down again. She carefully put the tips of her left index finger and thumb together to form a circle. Then she held up her pointer finger of her right hand and shoved it through the circle.

I had no idea what she was doing and I was getting tired of trying to guess. Her eyes got big and she leaned in, expecting me to have the secret all figured out.

"Don't you get it?" she asked, frustrated with me. "Get what?" This was harder to figure out than it should be.

"The secret!"

"About Tom?"

"Seriously, Anna, you make everything so difficult."

She had no choice but to tell me or let it go. "I don't know what the secret is," I said in frustration, unable to guess what she so badly wanted to share.

"Jolene? Tom?" She was hinting again.

My first thought was how happy Jolene was, and how grumpy Tom seemed.

"What about them?" This wasn't going the way she wanted.

"Oh good grief, Anna, don't you learn anything at school?" I stopped to think that I learned all kinds of things at school, but obviously not the same things as Sally.

Once again she did the little finger action, pointing at the picture of Tom. "Jolene has the hots for Tom and he has the hots for her."

""Why?" I asked and then reminded her, "Tom is Sandy's boyfriend!"

"Well Jolene said he is going to break up with her."

My eyes grew as big as full moons while I struggled with a response.

"They are doing it," Sally continued.

"Doing what?"

"You know, the nasty bump that I told you about."

I remembered what she had told me about. If she was telling me the truth, it was that thing parents do in the privacy of their bedrooms. That thing that I was never going to have any part of.

"That's gross," I added. "Tom is eighteen, and Jolene is only thirteen."

"Jolene doesn't say it's gross," Sally let out a silly little laugh, "and she will be fourteen in January."

I didn't want to listen to this any longer and decided it was time to leave Ellen's room and get some fresh air. As I passed through the living room, my parents raised their eyebrows and smiled at me, reminding me that I had a head full of curls. At least that was one good thing.

Outside, I sat on the swing so I could think. I wasn't sure if Sally was making things up or if her little secret was the truth. What I did know is that I needed to read Ellen's diary as soon as possible. I hoped that the answers would be in her handwriting.

~ *Chapter 25* ~

After everything Sally had shared with me, I was eager to go into Ellen's bedroom to read her diary. But, I needed Sally and Ellen out of the house. I often knew where Ellen was, but Sally was harder to keep track of.

It was Saturday morning and Ellen had come home from Sandy's to change before leaving for work. I was still uncertain with what to believe, but I sure wasn't as excited about Jolene with Tom as Sally seemed to be. Sally had a strange way of looking at things. It was also true that she was changing. I noticed she was growing up and trying to act older. Even her body was changing, which included "curves in all the right places" like I had heard Sandy and Ellen joke about. I also thought about how Jolene was already thirteen, going on fourteen, and that Sally was becoming interested in things that were different from what we used to do together. I was feeling left behind.

When I had finished my breakfast, I went outside to play. It wasn't long after that Sally came bouncing down the steps. She ignored me as she got on her bike. I shouted to her, "Where are you going?" I may have sounded a little too excited to see her leaving.

"None of your business!" she hissed.

"What's your problem?" I asked as I had no idea why she wasn't being more pleasant. It was morning, after all, and she was always as bright as sunshine that time of day.

"I don't have a problem, okay?" She was straddling her bike, her feet planted on both sides when I raced up to her for an answer, and more importantly, to find out how long she would be gone.

"I'm just wondering where you are going." I just hoped she tell me.

"I am not taking you with me!"

"I don't want to go with you." I stood there looking at her wondering why her mood was so sour. I had been noticing her unpredictable moods lately and could only assume it had to do with growing older.

"Good, then bug off! I'm going to Jolene's house."

I didn't say anything more, but didn't understand why she wasn't in a better mood if she was going to hang out with her friend.

"Well have fun and tell Jolene hi," I called after her, almost too happy. She mumbled something that I couldn't understand and I skipped back into the house.

With both Sally and Ellen out of the way, I climbed the stairs to the landing. I stood there for a moment to feel the silence. Ellen's door, of course, was closed tight. I always felt a little bad when I would sneak in, but I also convinced myself that I wasn't really snooping through her things.

I stood there, working up the courage to enter. That was always the hardest part because there was always a chance of getting caught. But once I was inside her room and the door closed behind me, in my mind, I became Ellen Marie Hendricks.

I looked around the room. Ellen's fan was braced in the window, blowing on high, with magazine pages fluttering from the breeze. I sat down on her bed and was embraced by a magical moment.

Everything was so quiet except for the fan, and time seemed to have slowed down. Besides my closet, this was the best room in my house. I noticed everything was neat and tidy, as always. I reminded myself that once I got off her bed, I would be sure to straighten the covers so there was no trace of me.

On the vanity was her comb and the yellow ribbon that she had worn on her date the night before. I walked over to touch the soft, silky ribbon, and then looked at myself in the mirror. I still had some loose curls from the night before, but my sleep had flattened most of what Sally had created. Still, I pulled my hair into a ponytail and wrapped the ribbon around it. I tried to bounce my ponytail the way Ellen would, but he ribbon slipped out, slowly falling to the floor. I carefully picked it up and put it back on her vanity.

After a moment of taking in my surroundings, I reminded myself why I was there. I opened the bottom drawer and found the diary at the very bottom of the pile, right where it was the last time I read it. I pulled it out and sat down on the floor.

Taking a deep breath, I carefully opened it up and glanced once again at the page I had read previously. Ellen had been busy writing because many more pages were filled up.

Tuesday, May 28, 1968
Dear Diary,

Well, things are looking up because Sandy grabbed me after second hour and said she had gotten the curse. Thank goodness! I still said I could get pills for her. She isn't convinced I should be taking them. I have to admit I feel a bit bad, but the alternative is worse. Things are iffy with Tom. I don't know what he could want! Sandy is beautiful, delightful, and popular. I wish they got along as well as Greg and me. Tom will graduate the end of the week. Sandy thinks he is depressed about not being accepted to college to play football. Well, I'm looking forward to a wonderful summer vacation and hopefully things work out for them. Sandy will always be my best friend.

Later....

I couldn't see where that said much about Sally's secret. Except Tom wasn't a good boyfriend. I kept turning pages, pausing to think. Maybe Ellen and Sandy had no idea about Jolene and Tom. If that was so, then maybe I wouldn't find what I was looking for. Still, reading her diary was thrilling, so I continued.

Saturday, June 1, 1968
Dear Diary,

At last we are out of school. I'll be a senior in August! I can't believe it. All of us went to Tom's graduation and his party. I have no idea what's next except the draft is looming for him. The war is real and the boys who have no choice are anxious. Something is not right for Sandy and Tom, but neither of us can put our finger on it. Graduation is supposed to be an exciting time, but his dreams of college football fell apart. Another reminder to study hard and get good grades. Tom was a little too into sports and parties to study, it seems.

I worked today which was fine. Sandy has me thinking about the pill. I know what I'm doing isn't the best idea, but I am not really

120 LINDA M. JAMES

stealing, as I told her. I put two dollars in the cash register each time. I have to really think about this. In the meantime, it's summer vacation and I couldn't be happier. It's time for the beach, dates, friends and fun!

More to come……

E

Ellen's diary suggested that Tom is unhappy because he wasn't going to college, or that he might be drafted. Or maybe he realized that Jolene was too young and that he wasn't the nicest person to Sandy. But nothing about Sally's secret. Having these thoughts made me upset with Tom. I really didn't like him anyway, but now I was sure.

As I was sitting on Ellen's floor, the phone rang, startling me. I closed the diary and returned it to the exact spot from where I removed it, and quietly closed the vanity drawer. I quickly looked around to make sure everything was in place, and then headed downstairs.

I quietly entered the living room when I heard my mother on the phone.

"You are so welcome, I'm glad you enjoyed it." My mother's voice sounded like it was dancing. I sat down on the cool floor behind a large stuffed chair so she wouldn't know I was there.

My mother continued, "You know, Leroy, I often cook too much and I would guess you are probably not eating the way a man needs to. I see no reason why I couldn't bring by some extras from time to time."

My father would be furious about this.

Shock caused my eyes to get big, and I leaned in closer to listen.. I know my mother was grateful Sally survived her incident, but I thought we should move on and forget about Mr. Leroy.

"Oh yes, I know, they are good kids and thank you for saying so," my mother said brightly. At least that was more than my father thought. As far as my father was concerned, I was nothing but a brat.

"Um, since I have you on the phone, I was thinking that maybe you'd think about, or consider…. Oh, heck, I guess I would like to invite you to church. God's house is always open for good servants."

What? For sure my father was going to blow a gasket.

"Well, I understand but give it some thought, and if I see you there, I'll introduce you to our pastor. Good-bye now." The phone receiver clicked.

I came out from behind the chair and started walking to the kitchen where my mother was now tending to baking. "Who were you talking to?" I asked. I seemed to have startled her as she jumped before she turned around.

"Oh, honey, I didn't know you were there." I guess the look on my face asked the question again as she answered, "Mr. Miller. He called to say he loved the pie, and would like to bring the dish back to me."

"Oh," I said softly. "Are you friends?"

"I'm doing what God's people should do. I'm being thoughtful of others."

"I don't think Dad will like that." Someone had to remind her as none of us needed my father slapping us around again, or yelling at us for doing things he didn't approve of. It all was still fresh in my memory.

"Your father needs to learn how to be thoughtful as well. Maybe I can be a positive role model, and show him how." I wasn't exactly sure what all of that meant, but in my heart I knew she was being a good person. I just didn't want any of us to make my father angry.

Her convincing him to think like her was going to be a big project, I thought, as I looked at my mother with a blank face.

"Here, have a cookie and go out and enjoy the day. She smiled warmly and handed me the cookie she had just baked.

Back outside I threw the ball on the garage roof for a while when all of a sudden from behind me, Sally snatched it. "When did you get here?" I asked with surprise as I had been so caught up processing everything I had just heard and read.

"Just now, dork!" She threw the ball hard at me.

"Stop it!" I threw it back at her, she dodged it and the ball went rolling almost to the garden. She giggled and plopped down on the cool grass and crossed her legs, her mood now improved.

"Too bad we can't go swimming. Jolene is going today." I didn't dare remind her *why* we couldn't go swimming. In a few days' time, our restriction would be lifted and we could get back to our daily trips to the pool.

I sat down next to her and asked, "Did Jolene talk about Tom when you were at her house?"

"Maybe!" She grinned at me like she might share something with me, or she might not.

"Well, *maybe* you were making things up about them, and *maybe* Jolene only has a crush on Tom, and *maybe* he doesn't even like her back!" I said all of it with too much sass, I realized afterward.

"Sheesh, are you calling me a liar?" Sally sat up straighter in defiance.

"No, I'm saying that maybe you are messing with me." I was staring hard at her.

"What's up your butt?"

"You!" I shot back. "I don't know if you are telling me the truth, and I feel bad for Sandy." I stood up to consider doing something else that didn't involve Sally, but continued staring at her.

"I don't know why you are mad at me because Tom and Jolene like each other. Good grief, I let you in on a little secret and you get all pissed off. Maybe you aren't grown up enough to handle the truth." Sally got up and stormed into the house.

"Fine!" I yelled after her, "You shouldn't swear." And the screen door slapped my words back at me.

~ *Chapter 26* ~

It was Monday and the first day of Vacation Bible School. Everything was looking brighter. It was finally going to be a good week. Our ban on swimming was over and now VBS was here.

It was the middle of June and the summer sun was boiling. Sally was putting up with the whole idea, thinking that she was too grown up to attend VBS, but it was her last year. VBS was for kindergarten through sixth grades. Sally's attitude about almost being a teenager was emerging faster than I could keep up with. She wouldn't turn thirteen until February, but she was already anticipating it by saying, "I'll no longer be a kid in the space of one day".

I could see that she was being pulled from a place that was a kid like me, to a place that was unfamiliar to both of us. Sally was talking about boys and friends, and I wasn't included unless she wanted me to be.

It didn't matter to me what Sally thought about VBS, I loved it. My mother packed our lunch every day and would stand in the driveway, waving at us, saying, "Be safe, and have fun!" And we would race our bicycles out of the driveway, filled with excitement. After all, it was one full week of games, recreation and crafts. I couldn't think of a better way to learn about God.

When we returned home from VBS in the afternoon, we would quickly change and go to the swimming pool for a few hours before supper. Yes, things were definitely looking up with no more sitting around the house hearing about silly secrets that I still wasn't sure about.

The first three days of VBS were identical. We'd race to get there, have fun, and then race home to get changed for swimming.

But Thursday was different.

We had gotten to church and did all the same things we had done the days before, but today was anything but identical. The wind had picked up and it seemed a storm was brewing. As things were winding down for the week, everyone was getting tired, teachers included. Whatever storm was in the air was also breaking loose in Danny Parker.

He and Sally had been warned throughout the day to leave each other alone. I had heard a couple of the teachers sternly say, "Sally and Danny, please stop it and pay attention."

This particular day was starting to feel more like regular school than Vacation Bible School, where usually there were no conflicts. Earlier in the day, at recess, Danny had pushed Sally so hard she nearly fell. She wasn't happy about it either because she let him know the rest of the day just what she thought of him by calling him names at every chance.

I was ignoring their spat because it made me feel uncomfortable. At the end of the day, when it was time to head home, both Sally and I were on our bikes, ready to push off, wasting no time so we could get to the swimming pool.

I should not have been surprised when Danny came running over to Sally and said, "You think you are so grown up, calling me names." I started feeling more heat from fear than the air. There was now no adult supervision.

Sally was not going to back down, which I should have known. She was fearless, and shouted back at him, "Go away you little turd." Sally had her right foot planted on the pedal of her bike and the other foot on the ground, holding tight to the handle bars. I was doing the same.

Danny didn't seem to like being called a little turd, because all of a sudden he grabbed her and pulled her to the ground. They both started slugging each other. I was so shocked that I was unable to move. I felt a hotness growing inside me when all of a sudden I dropped my bike, and marched right up to Danny Parker.

The heat inside gave me the courage to do the one thing I would not have thought to do. I pulled my arm back and, with tremendous strength, I unloaded the biggest punch I could to Danny's back.

I felt good about it until I found myself on the ground. Danny was quick to turn around and force a punch into the side of my jaw. Intense pain hit me like a brick and I cupped my face, trying to force the pain away.

"You dumb girl," his words almost pierced me worse than his punch.

Before he could hit me another time, Sally was on top of Danny jabbing both fists into his back, sides, and head. Not only could I feel the pain throbbing in my jaw, but I had the weight of both of them on top of me. I almost couldn't breathe.

Suddenly the heaviness eased and I could hear the familiar voice of Pastor Prewitt.

"Stop this right now! Get up, all of you," he said with a hardness I hadn't heard from him before. "This is not acceptable, especially at church, in the eyes of God, and in God's house."

"He's the one," Sally yelled, shaking a finger at Danny. "He started it."

"She's a troublemaker," Danny stared at Sally. "She has been teasing me all day. And her little sister pinched a nerve in my back!" He was thrusting a finger at me. I was feeling a different kind of heat now that was more like embarrassment than anger, as I noticed several other kids had gathered around to look on.

"No, you do not have a pinched nerve," Pastor Prewitt said, showing a hint of a smile. I hadn't seen him smile much, probably because being a preacher was a serious business.

Danny stood there with his fists still balled up, like he was ready to keep punching.

"It doesn't matter who, what or why this happened, but we need to get this right with God. We are going to pray." The creases in Pastor Prewitt's forehead scrunched together.

"We're not praying!" Sally shouted, her face was red hot. "We are going home to tell our mother. Come on Anna, right now, let's go," she ordered.

My mouth hung open, not believing what just happened. I was torn with what to do, but as I always did, I decided to follow Sally. I followed her away from the church, from the pastor and even away from God. None of it felt right.

As I jumped on my bike, Sally was already racing down the road. I tried but couldn't catch up to her, my legs burning in the attempt. My lungs were stinging and my jaw was aching. Pain seemed to be pulsing through my entire body.

I was puzzled by everything that had happened and now Sally had left me in the dust. I knew she was fueled by anger but I just couldn't keep up. Though I was hurting inside and out, I kept pedaling even though Sally was so far ahead of me.

When I got to the big hill, I had to get off, catch my breath, and push my bike uphill. I could see Sally fade over the top of it. She wasn't slowing down for me. I kept moving though tears were starting to blur my sight.

At the top of the hill I was able to take catch my breath again, mount my bike and start cruising to our street. Just as I got going at a good speed, closing the distance to my house, the wind grabbed me and I flew to the pavement face-first.

I didn't move for several moments, unable to understand what just happened, but I also knew that I needed to get into the house. As I stood up, my vision was even more blurry. I did my best to throw my bike off the road into the ditch, before managing the short walk home. I was trying to correct the blurriness, bringing both fists to my eyes, trying to rub sight back into them. I tasted blood and my hands felt wet.

I entered the house, blinking away the fuzziness and focusing my eyesight. I stood dazed before Sally and my mother, who instantly stopped talking.

My mother nearly tripped running to me.

"Oh my Lord, Anna, what did you do?" My mother was almost in tears at the sight of me and then I started sobbing. "Bike," was the only word I had enough strength to let out.

"She didn't look like that when we left church," Sally babbled so fast that she barely made any sense. My mother didn't respond to her comment and just stood there looking at me.

"We need to get you to Dr. Hatfield!" My mother's words sounded almost angry, which she rarely was. "I need to get my purse, so keep her away from the mirror and get a towel," she instructed Sally, who looked as shocked as I felt. Sally ran to the bathroom and came back with a towel.

My mother dabbed at the blood on my face, hands and knees.

"Come on, bring the towel with us," my mother insisted with urgency. And we quickly loaded into the Falcon. Sally, of course, jumped into the front but not before opening the back door for me.

Sitting in the back seat my eyes shifted back and forth from the bloody towel to the small rip in the seat, and then everything went black.

I woke up to a bright light and white sheet draped on a small bed with Dr. Hatfield looking over me.

"Anna, I need to get you cleaned up, and stitched. You've had a pretty bad fall on your face."

I didn't respond. I was aware that I had a bad fall, as the extreme aching in my jaw and my burning face were reminding me.

"Can you tell me what happened with your face and jaw?" he asked very calmly. Before I could open my mouth to speak, Sally started blabbering to him all about Danny Parker. I felt dizzy, like I might pass out again.

"Okay, Anna, let me get you comfortable." Dr. Hatfield took hold of my hand, not pressing for any more information.

"We need to do a couple of things," he said softly. "I need to extract the gravel and debris out of the abrasions on your face, and give you a couple of stitches, okay?" I nodded. "Once I do that, we need to take an X-ray of your jaw. I don't think it's broken or dislocated, but I just want to make sure."

Even though Dr. Hatfield was so sweet, his words caused me to start crying again. All of this was like a bad dream and I desperately wanted to wake up. I looked at my mother who had her hands over her face. Having noticed that, the doctor suggested she and Sally take a seat in the waiting room.

I was left alone in the little room with Dr. Hatfield and his nurse, Rosie. I felt scared, but Nurse Rosie was quick to see it and put her arm around my shoulders. She was a chubby grandma with more than one chin, and wore a white dress so stretched across her middle that the buttons were pulled tight. She had hands that were warm and soft like my mother's bread dough. And when she smiled at me, it felt like pulling curtains open to a bright sun.

"Anna, I don't want you to be afraid, but we need to fix you up," Dr. Hatfield assured me in the smoothest voice. I wondered if Sandy knew how lucky she was to have him as her dad. "You have a few things wrong, honey, and you are a brave young lady. Your lip has a little cut that needs a couple of stitches. Your nose isn't broken, but badly scratched. You have several skin abrasions. It's painful, I know! It's what we call road rash. Some of them are surface abrasions and some go deeper, so it's really important to clean those areas to avoid any infection."

As he was telling me all this, I was trying to breathe even more bravery into myself as not to cry over what pain the doctor and his kind nurse might cause. I noticed Nurse Rosie was getting out gauze and other supplies to start "fixing" me up.

"Okay, Anna, some of this won't feel nice, but it is necessary so that we can get you feeling better," Dr. Hatfield patted my hand. "Rosie is going to numb some of the area before I clean, sterilize, and stitch up your little cut."

"Anna, are you ready to be even braver than you've been?" I could tell the sweet nurse wasn't going to start tugging at my face until I was ready. I wanted Nurse Rosie for my grandma, if she would have me. I decided she was doing the right thing in life because I felt better just having her in the same room.

When I decided I was brave enough, I said as much by nodding my head yes.

"Here, sweetie, I have this teddy bear for you to hold onto if that would make you feel better," Nurse Rosie looked at me and handed me the stuffed bear.

Another head nod.

With that, Dr. Hatfield started cleaning my face with Nurse Rosie's help, as my lip grew numb. I had no idea that my face was going to be scrubbed worse than any bath time. Clutching the bear, I was certain the stuffing was going to come out. From the looks of it, some other kid had done the same thing as it was missing an eye.

My body stiffened as the doctor and his nurse kept working on my face, throwing bloody gauze pads into the trash. When my face was cleaned and stitched, ointment was applied and Nurse Rosie walked me to a dark room for a picture of my jaw.

After all the "fixing me up" was done, the nurse took hold of my hand, leading me to the waiting room. My mother jumped up and came running, throwing her arms around me; Sally right by her side, taking hold of my hand. "Oh, sweetheart, you already look better," my mother said with excitement. I still didn't know what I looked like, but if it was anything like how I felt, it wasn't good.

Dr. Hatfield came along shortly after. "Arlene, we took an X-ray of Anna's jaw and it's just a deep contusion. I'm sure it hurts, but it'll be fine. The rest is a good old case of road rash. I removed debris and she has two stitches by her lip."

He then removed a round yellow tin with a blue stripe on the top, from his white coat pocket. "This antiseptic ointment needs to be applied a few times a day to control the scabbing." He handed the tin to my mother and said, "She can come back and see me in about ten days and we will remove the stitches and see how she is healing." I cringed at the thought that I would need more pulling at my face.

"Anna, you need to take it easy for a bit, okay?" Dr. Hatfield had a huge, warm smile that felt like the summer air. I looked at him and smiled slightly in return, though it hurt, and barely whispered, "Okay." Before we left, Nurse Rosie put her doughy arm around me and told me I was such a good girl. I knew for sure, then, that I loved her.

My mother, Sally, and I walked to our car, climbed in, and headed home. "Anna, how did you fall on your face?" Sally leaned over the front seat to look at me. I wasn't much interested in talking to her as I started thinking about the fight at church and how I tried to keep up with her on my bike. Again, I was in a situation because of Sally's choices. I wanted to be angry, but I was just too sad and tired. "Fine, don't talk to me then," she left it at that and turned back around.

We pulled into the driveway and as soon as we got out of the car, my father came flying out the back door with Ellen trailing behind him. They both stood there staring like they no longer recognized me. My stomach became tangled up like I might get sick. I didn't want another beating, and then the tears became too heavy to hold back.

"What in the hell is going on, Arlene? What happened to Anna? Why was her bike lying in the ditch?" He jammed his thumb in the direction of my bike now in the grass, near the house. He was throwing out questions faster than anyone could answer.

"Calm down, Ivan!" My mother pressed her palms to her cheeks as if to calm herself.

"Don't tell me to calm down! My God, Arlene, look at that disfigured child!"

My mother took a deep breath before speaking, "Ivan, you are not helping the situation. Anna has been through a lot of trauma and needs us to deal with this calmly."

I wasn't feeling the slightest dose of calm. In fact, every bit the opposite.

"Does someone care to tell me what all this trauma is about." This was an order, not a question from my father. The sky that had been darkening all day was beginning to match my father's mood.

"Anna, maybe you should go lie down in your room as the doctor suggested," my mother's voice was as soft as velvet. I did as she said as I was feeling weak and tired, and didn't want to deal with this day any longer.

As I walked into the house, I could hear Sally start up about the fight with Danny Parker and the sight of me after my bike accident, to which my father said, "We'll continue this discussion in the house."

In my room, I lowered my aching body down on my bed, realizing that I was finally able to breathe in a normal way. I starting thinking about how so much could happen in such a short time. The entire afternoon seemed as long as one of Pastor Prewitt's sermons.

The next thing I knew Ellen was sitting on my bed, waking me up. I'd fallen asleep. At first I wasn't sure what day it was and or where I was.

"Anna, are you feeling better?" She was nearly whispering.

A big sigh escaped my mouth and I sensed the size of my lips were larger than they should be, however, my face wasn't burning as badly as it was earlier. I had yet to see my face, but according to my father I was disfigured. My heart was feeling heavy at the thought of growing up ugly.

"I'm okay, I think, but my face hurts." I responded.

"You've had a rough afternoon. Mom and Dad said that you and Sally will not be going back to the last day of VBS." Ellen sat there smoothing my hair away from ugly face.

"My lips feel huge," I said, "and dry."

"They are swollen is all. They won't stay that way. You can come down to join us for supper, but the doctor suggests a liquid diet for a few days." Ellen scrunched up her face as if hers was hurting as much as mine.

"A liquid diet?" I asked, licking my large lips.

"Yes, that means you need to drink from a straw, but only a couple of days."

I wasn't hungry anyway, but I sat up and looked at my hands and knees. They, too, had what the doctor called road rash. "Is my face going to be ugly forever?" I asked Ellen.

"No, you are going to heal. It looks kinda bad right now, but in no time at all it will seem as nothing happened." She stood up and took my hand to follow her.

I hoped she wasn't lying to me. We went downstairs to join my family for dinner, where I drank a glass of milk through a straw and no one talked about the accident. After we ate I would look at the face my father called disfigured.

Slowly approaching the mirror in the bathroom, my mother was right behind me to ease the outcome of what I would see. Most of the red abrasions were on the left side. My left cheek, my forehead, chin, nose and lips were all skinned worse than any knee or elbow I had ever seen.

It was bad enough that my face was skinned up but my eyes told more than my road rash. My deeply sad eyes said my face might heal, but my fractured heart was going to need more time.

Later in the evening, the sky broke loose and the storm that had threatened all day dropped rain as heavy as my heart.

~ *Chapter 27* ~

The next few days improved. I didn't know why a face filled with road rash would get so much attention, but it did. Friends, neighbors and church folks were calling to ask about me. Even Sally and Ellen wanted to spend time with me.

Nurse Rosie called me the day after the accident to see how I was doing and tell me that she and Dr. Hatfield thought I was a very brave girl. She said she looked forward to seeing me again in a week or so, and reminded me that my mother was to continue putting ointment on my face and lips.

My fist fight and bike accident was becoming a big deal, but per my father's stern orders, my appearance outside our home was to be limited. I wasn't able to go to the swimming pool, the park, downtown, or church. "No one should be gawking at your face, the way it looks right now," he claimed.

He also made it clear to me and Sally that he didn't want anyone talking about how his daughters got into a fist fight with a boy. Not only with a boy, but on the church property. "What a disgrace," he'd said a few times after it happened. While my sisters and mother were finding endless ways to tend to me, my father acted as though I wasn't there. I assumed he didn't like the way I looked. I didn't blame him, I didn't like the way I looked either.

Two days after my accident Ellen and Sally came home from shopping. Ellen handed me a bag. "What is it?" I jumped up with surprise. "Well open it up, it's something to cheer you up." She was right, I could use a little cheering up.

Inside the brown paper bag was a Barbie Doll with brown hair with a hot pink ribbon attached. She was dressed in a green, orange, and pink striped pleated dress, and hot pink shoes.

"I can't believe it!" I said, setting the Barbie down and then throwing my arms around Ellen's neck, thinking she was the best sister.

I was smiling so wide, my lips felt sore from being stretched, but I didn't care. Next, Sally said, "Here you go," and handed me her surprise — a color book and a box of Crayola 48! I squeezed her too. Being confined to the house was one thing, but now I had something new to play with.

Later on Saturday evening, Greg came to pick up Ellen. I was sitting outside waiting for him, like I always did whenever he and Ellen were going somewhere. I loved having him come to our house. As he pulled into the driveway, I ran up to greet him. He waved as he put the car in park. Getting out, he smiled at me, his dimples growing deeper.

"Sorry about your accident, squirt," he said, handing me a candy bar.

"Thank you," I smiled back at him. I wasn't sure what it was, but Ellen and Greg together made me feel so happy.

"You sure took a tumble, huh?" Greg ruffled the top of my head.

"Yeah, but I'm getting better!" I said to him, even though it had only been a couple of days.

"Well, I'm glad to hear that!" He lifted his chin towards the house, asking, "Is that sister of yours ready?"

I smiled up at him again, and said, "Come on in, I think she is, but I'll check." I led Greg inside to wait as I raced up the stairs to get Ellen. Her door was open and I watched her double checking her face and clothes. "Greg's here!" I announced, standing in her doorway. "Okay, how do I look?" Ellen asked. She was wearing navy-and-white-plaid pedal pushers and a white, sleeveless blouse. Her hair was pulled into a ponytail, and tied with a navy ribbon.

"You look beautiful," I responded, because I really thought she did. She smiled and we both went downstairs.

Obviously Greg thought Ellen looked beautiful, too, because his smile grew large and his eyes sparkled like diamonds as she entered the living room.

"You look fabulous, Ellen!" He stood, gleaming at her, then planting a tender kiss on her cheek. "Ready to go?" Greg asked, taking her hand to guide her out to his car after they said their good-byes to my parents. I ran after them to watch them leave.

"Be good, squirt," he said, winking at me as he closed Ellen's car door.

~ *Chapter 28* ~

It was Sunday morning and I didn't have to go to church because of my face. I watched my family, including my father, drive off without me, and waved after them. I decided I wasn't going to miss listening to Pastor Prewitt go on about praying and being a good servant. It wasn't often that I was allowed to be home alone, but this was an exception and I was quite thrilled.

After my family had left, I went into the bathroom to look at my face to see if it was getting better. I had been checking frequently since my accident. It had only been a few days, but I decided that I was healing a little bit and my lips were not as big as balloons anymore. Plus, I didn't have to drink from a straw any longer. Yes, things were better but still my face was red and scraped up along with some bruises.

I went outside to swing. The morning air was thickening up, but I figured if I was pumping back and forth, the breeze would cool me off. I pushed my legs back and forth listening to the creaking sound of the rope.

It reminded me of when my father put the swing up for us. I was five years old when I sat watching him on a ladder, tying the rope around a sturdy branch. He was dressed in khaki pants and a sleeveless undershirt, most likely aiming to keep as cool as possible in the summer heat. His arms were tanned and muscular as he moved the ropes around the branch just so, insuring safety.

I was entranced when he took an old board, drilled four holes in it, threaded rope through, and stated, "Girls, I've got a surprise for you!" He had the look of a kid himself, full of smiles. "But this swing is for all of you and there will be no fights over it, or it comes down."

The three of us looked at each other with big, happy grins and said, "We will never fight about it, Dad!" I guess we valued the swing too much to ever lose privileges, so we never really had many spats within earshot of our father.

Ellen did have a few rules of her own, however. "When I have

Sandy over, you two better make like a banana and split," she was fond of saying, but rarely did she enforce anything with too much authority. Now five years had passed, Ellen was grown up and not interested in swinging anymore, and now it looked like Sally was soon going to be too grown up as well.

I delighted in the fond memory but now I slowed down enough to drop out of the swing and roll in the cool grass.

I was flat on my back, looking at the shape of light on the trees over me, while enjoying the grass on my arms and legs. I felt a little guilty that I wasn't in church but it was with good reason that I wasn't.

I thought many times how God is everywhere, not just church. I looked up at the sky, the white clouds were fluffy, like cotton balls. The sun was surrounded by a soft haze and the birds were singing something joyful. I got lost in the sights and sounds of all that surrounded me and I was sure that God was right here in this very moment.

But then a shadow fell over me, and shaking me from my moment with God was a throaty voice, "Is your mother home?" I looked up to see Mr. Leroy standing there.

I swiftly sat up and tried to find my voice, realizing Mr. Leroy's face twisted up when he looked at me, and then he rubbed his chin, seeming confused. His mouth was shaped into an oval like he was now trying to find his voice, too. All of a sudden, I realized he was surprised by my face and I looked away.

I cleared my throat while looking down at my hands, and said, "She's at church."

"Oh, of course. Ah, well, I wanted to return her pie plate." He clearly was uncomfortable, and I was anxious. I had been so excited to stay home alone and now I had no one to protect me in case Mr. Leroy really was a pervert.

I gulped as I stood up. My heart was bouncing around in my chest like a captured butterfly.

"Looks like you had an accident of some sort!" He pointed to my face, his voice quickly replacing the silence.

I briefly glanced at him and nodded. I didn't feel like explaining the whole incident, certain my father wasn't keen on others knowing what happened, especially the part about fighting with Danny.

"Well, could you give this pie plate back to your mother?" he continued, attempting to push away the awkwardness. I nodded again. "Um, looks like you need to take it easy, kid," he cautioned as he turned and walked to his truck.

It felt like I had been holding my breath as I let out an enormous sigh of relief when he left. As he backed out of the driveway, I ran into the house with the pie plate. I decided to spend the rest of the morning inside the house waiting for my family to return from church. And while I did that, I decided it was best to let my mother know about the pie plate when my father wasn't around. None of us wanted to listen to another one of his rants.

~ *Chapter 29* ~

Later in the day Sandy came over to hang out with Ellen. She brought me a stuffed bear and a 'Get-Well-Soon' card. My accident and damaged face were sure producing a lot of attention.

"Anna, I heard you took quite the fall the other day." Sandy sweetly smiled at me and patted my shoulder. "I hope this little present makes you feel better. My dad says hi."

I felt the corners of my mouth turn up at the thought of Dr. Hatfield. Sandy was a fortunate girl, except having Tom as her boyfriend.

"Thank you, Sandy," I smiled back at her though I was certain she thought my face was a mess. Then the two girls went up to Ellen's bedroom.

A short time after they had climbed the stairs, I took my new bear up to my room, set it on the bed, and started changing my new Barbie's outfit.

I could hear Ellen and Sandy laughing across the hall. I stood in my doorway and noticed the the door to Ellen's room was open a crack. The temptation to sit outside the door and listen was pulling at me until I couldn't fight it anymore.

I quietly sat down outside her room, near the opening.

More laughter.

"Well, tell me, do you think you'll get married some day?" Sandy asked with a teasing tone. "You know, high school sweethearts do get married!"

"Who knows, I really want to have a career so I need to focus on studying, but I do really like Greg! A lot!" Ellen gushed and then paused as if she was really thinking this over, then changed the subject, "What about you and Tom?" Ellen asked, "Where are things with you two?"

"I don't know. He's a tough one to figure out. He's been arguing with his dad about his prospects of going to college. He also thinks he will be drafted as he is young, healthy and strong. Not to mention his dad pressures him about working around the farm. I don't know, but I think his dad is more upset about college than Tom, and that's saying a lot."

"Hmm," Ellen added. "Is his dad upset he can't avoid the draft, or because of not being accepted into college?"

Sandy answered, "I don't really know or understand all of it. And, as far as me and Tom, something hasn't been right for a while. I don't know, like maybe he is interested in someone else. Or he is just depressed. I guess he just isn't a man of many words."

I cupped my hand over my mouth to hold in a gasp.

Maybe Sally was telling the truth! My eyes lit up like fireworks on the Fourth of July. *Poor Sandy! How can I say anything to Ellen about Sally's secret?*

I was torn with a feeling like choosing one friend over the other and no matter the choice, someone was going to be hurt.

Guilt was building in me and I didn't want to listen any longer, so I went outside to swing and think. All my thoughts were getting muddled. I had knowledge of something bad, but was sworn to secrecy. No matter what I did, either Jolene or Sandy was going to be hurt, and I liked them both.

I was also struggling with the fact that my father was so disappointed with me and my mangled up mess of a face. I had been feeling like he noticed me less since my accident. I sighed in frustration. There wasn't much I could do about any of it.

I decided to try and push away the bad thoughts, remembering all the gifts and attention I was getting lately. I was happy that people cared about me, but I wanted my face to look like it used to.

Just as I was feeling sorry for myself and trying to shake off the bad thoughts, my father pulled the Galaxie into the garage, got out and shouted to me from the driveway, "Anna, I've got something for you." Then he went back into the garage and came out carrying a cardboard box.

Confused, I stopped swinging, and slowly moved in the direction of the driveway. *What could he possibly have for me?*

My father approached me when I hesitated to move any closer. He set the box down, and I could hear scratching and movement inside. Then I heard a yip.

"Go on, open it," he encouraged me.

I ran over to the box, pulled back the flaps and there inside looking up at me was a scruffy, blond puppy. As soon as I pulled out that wiggly little puppy, I let out a shout of delight which caused my mother and sisters, along with Sandy, to come running outside to see what the squeals were all about.

"Just something to cheer you up," my father said, looking at me with a smirk. "You've had a rough time of it." I could tell from his big grin, he was quite proud of his good gesture.

In my shock, I set the little puppy down and I went up to my father and said, "Thank you, Dad, I love him!" And then I surprised myself and gave my father a big hug while the fluffy little puppy danced around my feet. For this one moment, I felt that maybe my father did love me.

"It's a female, Anna," he corrected me.

"Oh, ha, she is so cute and tiny."

"Wow, a real live dog!" Sally came running over to pick up the little fluff ball. "She has fur the color of sand. You could name her Sandy." Both Ellen and Sandy looked at each other laughing, and said at the same time, "No, I don't think so!"

Happiness filled my heart up with so much love for this happy little creature that I was reminded how I felt about Nurse Rosie when I announced without hesitation, "Her name is Rosie!"

I sat down next to the puppy and said, "Rosie, you are my best friend!" She jumped on me like she was telling me the same thing, and we all giggled at the frisky little puppy.

"Just keep in mind, Anna, she is a responsibility," my father added. "She needs to be taken care of, but all of us will help, right, gang?"

I couldn't believe my good fortune. My terrible accident was turning out to be the kind of blessing Pastor Prewitt would make into a sermon: "Take heart, some disasters will turn into blessings."

~ *Chapter 30* ~

I t was a couple of weeks after my accident and my mother said there was no reason to stay out of sight any longer. My scars were healing up, now only pink splotches on my face. I was feeling hopeful that my ugly scars would disappear completely and I'd look like I used to.

I had been playing outside with Rosie when my mother came out with her handbag hanging from her arm, indicating she was off on some errand. I didn't bother to ask if I could go along, but instead, she called to me, "Anna, sweetheart, do you want to go to the grocery store with me?" I felt my smile grow as wide as the Grand Canyon, and I went running up to her. "I guess you do," she beamed back at me. "But put Rosie in the house first."

I scooped up little Rosie and placed her inside as my mother instructed, then raced back to the driveway. Just as I was closing the door of the front seat, Sally came running outside toward the Falcon. She opened the front door indicating that I should move to the back.

"Now Sally, this is a special outing for Anna, so you can sit in the back this time!" My mother's voice was firm and decisive. "It's only right that you start sharing the front seat once in a while," she added.

Sally grumbled but did as she was told. I was so happy that I couldn't help but smile the entire way to the Red Owl store. Once the car was parked, Sally and I raced into the air conditioned store, waiting for our mother to catch up to us. We did this every time.

I loved going to the grocery store to look at all the wonderful food choices and inhale the special smells. Every week my mother would take her list as long as my arm and carefully check it while she pushed a cart up and down every aisle. Sometimes she didn't move along quickly enough, getting caught up comparing items, which made no sense to me.

Today was a day like that. We were standing right in front of dozens of jars of peanut butter, and my mother was having trouble deciding which one she was going to buy. She seemed far away in thought because she didn't even hear her name until I pulled her sleeve.

"Yoo-hoo, Arlene," called Florene Dahlberg, almost trotting towards us too quickly, which I concluded was not good because she was old enough to be a grandma. But finally my mother put the jar back on the shelf and turned to Mrs. Dahlberg, saying, "Hello, Florene."

Howard and Florene Dahlberg were members of our church. Every Sunday they'd prance all the way to the front of the church where Mr. Dahlberg let his wife go in ahead of him. Their pew was the third one back from the front, on the right side. No one else thought to sit there, not even Danny Parker's family who was forever on the search for the right one.

Howard Dahlberg was the president of First Choice Bank and they lived on Wellington Drive. Every year they purchased a new car from my father and every summer my father would say the same thing, "The Dahlbergs are coming in soon to buy a new car from me, as sure as the sun is going to rise and set."

And sure enough that is what happened. Just a few weeks earlier my father announced at dinner, "Howard and Florene bought a brand new '68 customized Thunderbird! What a car! They wanted the works and I delivered!" It was obvious what made my father happy. When he talked about Fords, he turned into someone anybody would like. He was expressive, joyful and actually a nice person.

As I was standing there thinking about what kind of peanut butter we were going to get, Mrs. Dahlberg bent down to put her face close to mine, saying, "Do you know how lucky you are to have such a happy and fun daddy?" Her bright pink lips stretched wide.

The question caused me to wonder if she was talking about the same person I knew. If she was, she'd be surprised. But then I remembered how giddy he was when he talked about selling cars. No wonder Mrs. Dahlberg thought he was someone he wasn't.

Her dark hair was styled like Laura Petri on the *Dick Van Dyke Show,* and she smelled like Aqua Net. I was rather certain nothing could mess up that hair of hers.

Breaking my trance, she looked straight at my mother and said, "Oh goodness, Arlene, your baby really did have quite the accident, huh? Ivan told us all about it and he was so worried she would be disfigured for life." Florene Dahlberg clutched her hand to her heart as if it was beating too fast.

"Well, as you can see, she is healing up nicely." I noticed my mother's voice was soft and wispy. I knew that my mother wasn't all that fond of Mrs. Dahlberg, and even called her a busy-body from time to time.

But my mother's body said more about her opinion than her words. She had stated to my father on more than one occasion that Florene Dahlberg was a fake, to which his response was always the same, "Just remember, Arlene, the Dahlbergs contribute to all your finery, so treat her nice."

"I know, but what a scare to have the skin torn right from her face." This comment made my mother tense up and stand taller, but Mrs. Dahlberg kept on, "You have such a beautiful family that I can't imagine this kind of thing happening to such a good looking bunch."

I could understand why my mother wasn't thrilled with the woman. I looked back at the peanut butter again and wished we'd get on our way, but the two women kept on chatting, or at least one of them did and the other nodding in response.

Just then I decided I had heard some of the oddest conversations between adults right here at the grocery store. With that thought and my boredom, my memory drifted back to another conversation that also took place at the Red Owl.

Ellen had just become a teenager and my sisters and I were helping my mother with the grocery shopping when crabby, old Mrs. Morris came up to us. She wore a permanent scowl. "Well, Arlene, I see your girls are growing like weeds!" She was standing in the cereal aisle, and there was no avoiding her.

"Hello, Hazel," my mother had said reluctantly, sounding like she wished she was invisible. "Yes, Ellen just turned thirteen last week!"

The corners of my mother's mouth slowly turned upward after

she said it, but then that smile slipped away just as soon as it appeared.

I could tell my mother just wanted to get about her shopping. However, Mrs. Morris was intent on telling her that she sure would have her hands full now that we had a teenager in the house.

"Oh good grief, Arlene, I tell ya, those boys of ours were about the death of me!" Mrs. Morris shook her head in disgust. "They practically ate us out of house and home, were always up to mischief, and our Timmy wrecked the car! More than once!" She paused a moment, seeming to reflect on how bad her sons were, and continued, "He's lucky he didn't wreck his noggin! He was the worst of the bunch." She knocked her knuckles against her forehead, but she wasn't done, "No, I wouldn't go back through those years for nothing. Three teenage boys at one time?" She said it like a question but wasn't looking for an answer, and continued talking, "No thank you, that was the worst. Let's hope you have an easier time, Arlene!"

My sisters and I had stood there looking at Mrs. Morris wide-eyed. And, not surprising, my mother responded in a way only she could, "Well, Hazel," she sighed and snapped her purse shut, looking as though she needed to keep her hands busy, and continued, "I expect the girls will be just fine, with some anticipated bumps here and there, but I trust we'll get through and..."

Before my mother could finish Mrs. Morris interrupted, "Well, I suppose it is true that girls are a lot less trouble than boys. If so, you should have an easy time of it. Good to see you, Arlene." And then she turned to me and my sisters, and said in a gruff voice, "You girls behave yourselves so your mother doesn't have to go through hell like I did!" Not one of us knew how to respond to that comment so we just stood there and watched her stroll away.

It was now a few years ago that Ellen had turned into a teenager, and Sally was fast approaching thirteen. We'd have two teenagers in our house and I was hopeful that my parents would be spared the horrible teen years that Mrs. Morris had.

Snatching me from memory lane was Mrs. Dahlberg telling me to be a good girl for my parents and, "Be careful on that bicycle, young lady."

Perhaps Mrs. Morris was right. Maybe I was shaping up to be like Timmy Morris as I almost wrecked my noggin', too, in my accident. And with Sally's incident, maybe we were destined for as much trouble as the Morris boys. Who could know?

I had been excited to go out in public to the grocery store, but now I wasn't so sure. It seemed that grown-ups were sometimes just as mean as kids. I couldn't help but wonder how adults could pierce the heart of a child with such little effort. The kids at school would often say, "Sticks and stones will break my bones, but words will never hurt me." That sure didn't make any sense because didn't people know that words could shatter a heart, and bones could always heal?

After our odd conversation at the Red Owl, we drove quietly back home, with Sally in the front seat after she pushed me out of the way so she could be the first one to the car.

At home, Sally and I helped my mother carry in groceries and we were greeted by happy little Rosie, who came rushing up to us at the door.

So what if I felt deflated from both Mrs. Dahlberg and Mrs. Morris? It was Rosie who filled my heart with love and maybe she was the one I could trust the most.

~ *Chapter 31* ~

The Fourth of July was three days away and the temperatures were rising. It was blistering hot. The tradition of the holiday was to attend a parade downtown complete with floats, fire trucks, pretty girls in convertibles and men in uniforms. My favorite part was the candy that was tossed to the curb while all the excited children raced to pick it up. Sally loved to prove she could collect more than me, and tease that maybe she'd share if I was on my best behavior.

Later in the day, my father would grill hamburgers and hotdogs, and we'd play croquet, which meant that the day before Sally and I would have to mow the grass. "Girls, the yard needs to be pristine if we are going to have a championship game," he beamed, sounding like a happy dad. "The garden needs weeding and watering, too," he added, briefly taking the excitement out of me.

At dusk, we'd gather in the family car and venture off to see the fireworks. I loved this time of year. It felt like the kind of happiness we shared at Christmas.

Every year my parents' friends, Gary and Minnie Ehlers, and Wayne and Gladys Thompson would come to our house for the barbecue. They all would sit in lawn chairs on our patio. The men drank beer while the women mostly drank lemonade, except Mrs. Ehlers. She was known to be fond of whiskey. Sometimes they all played croquet, but mostly the men would take part in the game.

This year Ellen had invited Greg, Sandy and Tom to our family gathering, which meant our day would be a lot more fun. In years past, we'd invite different friends, but it seemed that Sandy had been coming to our house every year that I could remember.

The first few days of July were spent weeding, watering, and mowing the grass in order to have the place spruced up for our celebration. Of course my father insisted on inspecting our work. After all, we were having company and he had said many times, "Our friends deserve to have immaculate conditions in which to celebrate!"

The Fourth arrived on Thursday, which started off with a big breakfast my mother had prepared for all of us. I was bursting with joy and couldn't wait for the parade. After Sally and I had eaten we went out to set up the croquet game so as "not to waste any time," Sally insisted. Little Rosie ran around the yard while we set up the game, acting as excited as we were.

"What color do you want this year?" Sally asked me. "You know Dad always wants black." The truth was, I didn't really care and I didn't like the color black anyway, so it didn't matter. But, it was true, for whatever reason, our father insisted that the black ball and mallet were his lucky color. I didn't want to point out that he wasn't exactly the winner very often so I wasn't convinced the color black was all that lucky.

"I don't care, but maybe yellow or orange," I said, thinking that those two colors reminded me of the sun and the moon, which I adored. I placed the last of the wickets in the ground. "Sally, do you think Jolene is coming over later today?" I decided to ask because now Tom was going to be at our house with Sandy, and the thought of them together was starting to feel very awkward to me. "I don't know yet, but she might. Why?" She questioned me, looking around the yard as if inspecting it herself.

My eyes narrowed as I thought about how to answer. "Well, you know..." I looked up at the summer sky and then back at her, "Tom and Sandy are going to be here, together."

"Well, you shouldn't worry about things that aren't your business, should you?" Sally glared at me, which told me I shouldn't say another word. "Since we have this all set up, I'm going to Jolene's for a little while and then we can go to the parade."

I decided to kill the time by throwing the tennis ball for Rosie. She had a lot of puppy energy and this was one way to tire her out. I figured out that if she was tired, she was less likely to be naughty. And, if she wasn't naughty, even my father was nice to her.

At noon, Ellen offered to drive me and Sally downtown to wait for the parade to start. My parents were going to get everything ready for our Fourth of July party that would immediately follow the parade. I hadn't been so excited since the day Rosie came to live with us.

And, just like every year, the same kinds of things happened: the candy, the floats, the pretty girls, the farm equipment, fire trucks, police cars and the like. This year, Tom was driving a tractor from his family farm. He looked quite proud. Ellen and Sandy stood on the curb waving to him as he passed.

After the parade, we climbed into the Falcon and brought Sandy home with us, meaning that Sally had no choice but to sit in back with me and point out how much candy she collected in a paper bag. "Anna, if you'd hustle a little, you could collect more. I just don't get how I always have more candy than you." She laughed, expecting me to laugh along with her.

"Sally, knock it off," Ellen yelled from the front seat. "This is not the day to be a brat." Both Ellen and Sandy looked at each other and smiled. I figured Sally must have been in a decent mood because she said nothing back to Ellen, for which I was thankful, as I didn't want to listen to the two of them bicker.

Once we got home, all the preparations had been made by my mother and father. On the kitchen table were red, white and blue napkins, paper plates and plastic forks and knives. Everything was ready for our guests.

My mother had also put Lays Potato Chips into a big bowl, sliced up buns for the burgers and hotdogs, and was at the stove stirring a pot of baked beans on low heat. My father was outside getting the charcoal grill started and loading up the cooler with beer and soda in anticipation of our guests.

First to arrive were Minnie and Gary Ehlers. Mrs. Ehlers was carrying a plate of chocolate chip cookies and a bottle of whiskey. Minnie Ehlers was wearing a tight red dress and red heels. "Hello, there, Ivan," she said enthusiastically. "I see you've got things under control and ready to go." She held up her bottle, smiling, "I'm ready to go too!" Both my father and Minnie laughed and laughed at this silly statement. Mr. Ehlers came waltzing over to my father, stretching out his hand to shake it. "Get yourself a beer, Gary!" my father ordered, while Minnie took her cookies inside to say hello to my mother.

I continued to play with Rosie while waiting for my favorite people to show up. I really liked my parents' other friends, Wayne and Gladys Thompson. Both were very nice people, especially Mrs. Thompson.

Soon everyone who was coming to our house had arrived, and our Fourth of July party was well under way. As the girls were trying to figure out who the first group of six croquet players would be, my father asked Tom and Greg if they were allowed to drink beer. "I am," Tom said quickly in response and went straight to the cooler to help himself. "I better pass, Mr. Hendricks," Greg said, and looked at Ellen like he was making the choice because of her.

"So, Tom, congratulations on your graduation!" My father slapped Tom on the shoulder. "What happens now?"

"Well, thank you, sir." Tom looked down at the ground and sighed before he looked at my father and said, "Well, I've been drafted and will ship out at some point, to an army base. Just waiting for my orders. I wish I were going to the University of Minnesota to play football, but I wasn't accepted." Tom gave my father a half-smile, though I was pretty certain it wasn't because he was happy about his future.

"I'm sorry to hear that, son." My father forced a smile in return and said, "I trust that doesn't set well with your Dad."

"Not much sets well with my dad, Mr. Hendricks." Tom drew in his lower lip with his teeth, appearing to push away enormous sadness that was trying to work its way out of him. I didn't know why, but for brief moment, my heart hurt for Tom.

"Well, let's not dwell on that kind of stuff today. Today is a day to celebrate." My father raised his can of beer to encourage everyone to be happy and said, "It's time I get the burgers and hot dogs on the grill!"

And, as my father had wanted, the day was joyful and everyone seemed to have a fun time playing croquet, playing fetch with Rosie, eating our fill of grilled hamburgers and hotdogs.

And, for this one day out of the year, happiness and laugher filled the gaps where sadness, loneliness or uncertainty settled in the hearts of so many.

~ *Chapter 32* ~

A week had passed since the Fourth of July and I had gone up to my bedroom to change into my swimming suit. The door was opened just a crack when I heard voices. "It's only until I have the baby and then I can come back home," Jolene's voice was slow and rhythmic. I leaned against the wall and moved my right ear as close to the opening as possible.

"How could you let this happen?" Sally asked, but didn't seem intentional in getting an answer as she went on asking questions, "When are you leaving?"

"Soon, probably by the weekend." Jolene sounded discouraged.

"I don't know how I will spend the rest of my summer without you," Sally raised her voice as if all of a sudden she was the one with a big problem.

Jolene sighed and continued, "Tom is really angry, so is my mom. It's a dumb mistake. And to think he cared about me!" Jolene sounded like she might cry.

I briefly squeezed my eyes shut and I covered my mouth with my hand. *Sally was telling me the truth!*

I thought about the day Sally and I sat in Ellen's bedroom and she told me about Jolene and Tom "doing it". The thought disgusted me now as much as it did then. Then I thought about how Tom didn't care about Sandy either. My thoughts were jumping around so fast, I couldn't keep up, but I kept on listening.

"Well, Tom is leaving and will be off fighting in Vietnam," Sally was trying to be reassuring, implying he really didn't have much say in the matter.

"I know," Jolene said. "But I will miss a large part of the school year and this whole secret can never be found out. That's why I have to stay with my aunt until the baby comes and the adoption agency takes over."

"How far is Des Moines, Iowa?" Sally asked.

"Too far," Jolene responded. "But, I will write to you, and you can write back."

"Well, what will you say when you come back and kids ask where you've been?" Sally pressed for more information.

"Good question and I guess I have several months to figure that one out."

"What about school in Des Moines?" Sally continued with questions.

"I guess my aunt knows someone who can tutor me and will come to the house."

All I could do was think about how awful this situation was. What I didn't know was exactly how awful it was going to get.

"Jolene, this is really terrible news. I will miss you," Sally sounded sincere. Both girls sighed, and I could hear the fear in Jolene's voice.

"I know, I'm really afraid," Jolene mumbled. She didn't sound like her usual, happy self anymore, and soon she'd be leaving town. She may have been Sally's friend, but I was going to miss her, too.

I didn't like Tom but he'd be leaving town as well and now my heart was breaking for Sandy. And Jolene.

"Does Sandy know about all of this?" Sally asked Jolene.

"They broke up!"

"What?" Sally's voice sounded like a loud chirp.

"They broke up a couple of days ago. He's being shipped out who-knows-when to some army base, and then on to Vietnam. And, now the whole pregnancy thing, he doesn't want anything to do with her, or me, it seems."

"Well if Sandy knows about you, she'll be mad as hell." Sally's voice was now more hushed.

"That's why the sooner I leave, the better."

"What a mess!" Sally added.

"Tell me about it."

There was a long silence between the two girls like they'd said everything they could think of when all of a sudden Jolene said, "Sally, I have something worse, to, ah...."

"To what?" Sally encouraged her to continue talking.

Again, I leaned in closer, straining to hear every detail.

"Um, this isn't easy, but I consider you my best friend," Jolene hesitated, and I heard a big sigh.

"Well spit it out then!" Sally was the queen of pulling out the darkest of secrets from about anyone.

"I don't know how to say this." Jolene was really stalling. I was beginning to wonder what could possibly be worse than being sent to live somewhere else, being pregnant and missing months of school.

"I won't tell a soul, Jolene." Sally's words sounded reassuring, but I wondered how long before she'd be sharing Jolene's secrets with me, even though I now stood at the door gaining information that I wasn't sure I should know.

And then, Jolene blurted out, "I am not sure if the baby is Tom's!"

"What do you mean? How can that be, Jolene?"

I could hear soft crying and sniffling.

"Jolene? Talk to me." Sally was really working to obtain more information.

"Who else are you talking about?"

"Sally, I am so confused and I don't know that I should say this."

"Well, you started, and I told you that I won't say a word!"

I could hear Jolene suck in an enormous amount of air before slowly letting it out. "My dad."

"What about your dad?" Sally pressured her to say more.

I was thinking the same thing Sally was asking. I thought her dad was sick and at the mental institution. I couldn't see what he had to do with Jolene's predicament unless he knew about her being pregnant and was angry like her mom.

Again, Jolene was working up courage to continue as the silence seemed to last too long.

"My dad was home a couple of months ago, before he had to go back to St. Peter. He is sick, Sally."

"So?"

"So, when he was home, he, you know....um," Jolene cleared her throat. Whatever she was trying to say was sounding very confusing and had nothing to do with going to Des Moines, Tom, or anything else the way I could see it.

"What are you trying to say?" Sally asked. "I'm getting confused."

"Oh, man, the baby might be because of my father."

My mouth fell open and my eyes felt like they'd pop out of my head. *What is she talking about?*

Sally seemed to channel my thoughts as that is exactly what she asked, "What are you talking about?"

"The whole bed-wetting thing is probably because of my dad. I don't like to think about it!"

"Well how is the baby connected to your dad?"

Then Jolene became angry, "He forced himself on me, Sally, okay? You happy now?"

Dead silence.

Then I could hear gut-wrenching sobs spilling out of Jolene. I didn't know what to do, and felt like I couldn't move. Thoughts were racing around in my head.

Oh dear God, is that what Dads do to their daughters?

I shook my head as if I could get rid of my horrible thoughts. I couldn't stand it anymore and quietly raced down the stairs, stretching over the squeaky step. I passed through the kitchen, trying to act normal, where my mother was working.

Slipping through the back door, I inhaled deeply and let it out before I raced to the back of the property to crawl inside of the secret cave.

I couldn't stop my rapid breathing or my dizzying thoughts. I thought I might pass out like I did after my bike accident, but instead, and to my surprise, I started weeping. The same kind of weeping I heard coming out of Jolene just moments before. My sobbing turned to gulping and my body heaved back and forth. I couldn't stop rocking back and forth, keeping time to my sobs. I remained curled up until my tears wouldn't fall anymore, and simply became sniffles. I plopped onto my back, feeling every ounce of energy drain out of me from crying. I remained there until I felt something cold on my cheek, and then licking my salty tear stained face.

My sweet Rosie.

"Come here, girl," I said to her, and then she lowered her little body next to mine and placed her head on top of my stomach. In a special moment, one little dog showed me that no matter what was happening, she loved me and would comfort me. I didn't know it was possible, but my love for Rosie kept growing.

~ *Chapter 33* ~

Enough time had gone by since I listened to Jolene tell Sally that she was expecting a baby, yet I was still in shock over the news. In a short period of time, things were unraveling quickly. Tom had broken up with Sandy, and she had cried to Ellen that she didn't understand. I had overheard her tell Ellen that Tom would soon be shipped off to fight in the Vietnam War, and that he felt it was best they end things. I wondered if Sandy and Ellen knew about Jolene. My guess was that they didn't.

"I knew things felt off," Sandy had said to Ellen. I had read that in Ellen's diary many times as well. I wondered how they could not see it coming, but then I knew more about the situation than I wanted to know, thanks to Sally, not to mention, overhearing things I probably shouldn't have. Still, I felt bad for everyone involved.

Now Jolene was living with her Aunt, Tom and Sandy weren't a couple anymore and summer was fading fast as we were halfway into July. School would start on August 28th, which meant that we only had about one month of summer vacation left.

There seemed to be a sadness all around as I knew Sally missed Jolene, but the two of them were writing letters back and forth. Sally would sit at the kitchen table with her stationery that she bought from Herman's Drugstore.

She'd write and write, and then spray the envelope with my mother's perfume, which I thought was weird. Then, we'd ask our mother if we could ride our bikes downtown to the post office and mail a letter to Jolene, which she always okay'd. I rather liked the idea that we were given the freedom to leave our neighborhood on a regular basis just because Sally was doing a lot of letter writing. It lifted her spirits and she was actually starting to look forward to school starting in August.

It was Thursday afternoon, and I was sitting on my bed cuddling with Rosie when Sally stood in the doorway of our bedroom, dangling an envelope pinched between her fingers.

"Look what I've got!" She was starting to sound like her old cheerful self.

"Let me guess, another letter from Jolene?" I asked but didn't expect an answer as I knew it was from her.

"I'm sure loving this pen pal stuff. I mean, I sure miss having Jolene down the street, but this letter exchange is really fun." Sally plopped down on her bed and ripped the envelope open and started reading silently. I didn't really need to hear what it said as Sally's facial expressions said enough.

Just as she was well into reading her letter and I was lazily snuggling with my puppy, a very angry Ellen threw our door open so furiously that it banged against the doorstop and slammed back into her.

Both Rosie and I jumped up to a sitting position. I couldn't possibly understand what had Ellen so upset, but she was glaring straight at Sally.

"How dare you!" Ellen snapped. I knew I was stuck where I was because Ellen wasn't moving out of the doorway. "Have you no sense of right and wrong?"

I felt Sally was too shocked to answer as she just sat there sizing Ellen up, no doubt wondering where she was going with this rant.

"I have no idea what you are talking about, or why you are bursting into my room. Get out!" Sally fumed back at Ellen.

"I will not!" Ellen stood firm. "How long did you know?"

"Know what? I have no idea what your problem is, but please leave, I'm busy." Sally went back to reading her letter which made Ellen more angry. She marched right up to Sally and grabbed the letter from her.

"Give that back right now!"

"What? Is this a letter from your little whore of a friend? Huh? The one who steals boyfriends and gets pregnant?" Ellen started reading the letter until Sally yanked it back, tearing it in two, leaving each girl holding one half of the letter.

"Now look what you've done!" Sally sounded near tears. I actually felt bad for her, but very uneasy that I was in the same room with these two angry sisters.

Ellen threw the torn half of the letter on the floor. "My best friend couldn't understand why her boyfriend was so withdrawn from her, but you sure knew, didn't you?" Ellen didn't allow any time for Sally to answer before she continued, "How long have you been keeping this little secret of yours?"

All of a sudden Sally looked over at me with a tightened jaw, scowling. I sat up straighter and pressed my back into the wall, not sure what she was trying to imply.

Then Sally looked at Ellen and back at me, as if we both were her enemies. Sally's voice hardened as she pointed a finger at me saying, "You should be mad at Anna, too! She knew about all of this! Everyone always thinks she is so innocent, well, she isn't! She didn't say anything about Tom and Jolene either!"

I felt my body pushing harder into the wall as if I could possibly escape from this quarrel. Ellen looked at me confused. "Anna?"

I gulped and felt trapped. I was on the verge of tears, too. I should never have listened to Sally.

Ellen continued, "Anna, is this true?"

I looked down at Rosie who was looking up at me with her dark eyes as if she was asking the same question, and all of a sudden my tears started falling. Ellen came and sat on the edge of my bed. Her anger had now softened. I could tell she wanted me to explain how I could possibly be harboring information, but didn't push it.

"Oh sure, poor little Anna isn't capable of doing anything bad," Sally grumbled.

"Sally, shut up!" Ellen barked at her.

"Seriously, Ellen, you are such a bitch, and so is Anna. You two deserve each other, thinking you are goodie-two-shoes. Well, guess what, you both are crazy."

Ellen stood up to face Sally, "Listen here, you are the one who is crazy, okay? You are the one who doesn't stop to think about who you hurt."

Ellen didn't wait around for a response and started walking toward the door when Sally screamed at her, "For your information, Jolene is my friend and I didn't say anything to you because I didn't want to *hurt her*!"

Ellen kept on walking, but then stopped and turned around, "Right, Sally! You just don't get it!" And she left our room with the door hanging wide open.

Sally ignored her as she started taping her letter back together.

As Sally did that, I slipped through the open door, leaving her alone with her letter, and took Rosie outside with me.

~ *Chapter 34* ~

As the long, lazy summer days passed, it seemed best that I keep my distance from both of my sisters. It also seemed to be working for the two of them not to speak to one another. Ellen didn't approach me again for answers after her fight with Sally. I was thankful as I didn't know what I could say to make any of it better.

The bottom line was that one terrible mistake was affecting the lives of many people. I didn't like Tom Ganley and I figured Sandy could find a nicer boyfriend, like Ellen had Greg. Sure, Sandy didn't deserve to get hurt, but maybe it was best that they broke up. He wasn't good for her, the way I saw things.

I was doing my best to enjoy my summer vacation, yet my thoughts would still return to the situation with my sisters and their friends, but the most disturbing was Jolene's dad. I didn't really want to know anything more about that situation, and still hoped and prayed that Sally wouldn't decide that I somehow needed to know all the gory details. I was done listening to her secrets.

The weekend was here once again and Ellen and Greg were now strictly going on solo dates since Sandy and Tom broke up.

It was a hot Saturday afternoon and Sally and I had gone to the swimming pool for a few hours to cool off. We came home in time for dinner like we always did but once we got home and placed our bikes in the grass next the house, I could tell something was wrong. Sandy's car was in our driveway, and so was Greg's.

Something felt off and I hesitated on rushing into the house. I stood there for a moment trying to figure out why I was feeling so uncertain when two of my favorite people were inside my house. Sally didn't seem to have the same tug at her feelings because she bolted into the house as she always did.

I slowly entered to find my parents, along with Sandy, Greg and Ellen sitting in the living room which was already a strange sight, but Sandy was devastated.

I stood in the arch between the kitchen and living room while Sally stood in front of the assembled group and asked, "What's going on?"

Greg and Ellen sat on both sides of Sandy trying to console her. Her face was red and flushed, and her eyes were filled with tears, which had obviously been spilling over her cheeks for a while.

I felt frozen in that archway. Something terrible had happened. I didn't know if I should enter or go back outside, but Sally asked again, "What's happening?" This question snapped all of them out of a spell of sadness that filled the room.

"Sally, I think you and Anna should go up to your room," my mother suggested, standing up and placing a hand on her back to nudge her towards the stairs. She motioned for me to come along, but as I started walking toward Sally and the stairs, Ellen stood up and said, "They probably should hear it now instead of later."

I felt my eyebrows scrunch together, questioning what could possibly be going on and if I really wanted to hear it, but Ellen went on, "It doesn't do any good to protect anyone from this news, it's going to travel like wildfire, and everyone in town is going to know shortly anyway."

I could not understand what was happening that could be so bad that my parents, sister, her friend and boyfriend would be sitting in my living room — the women in tears.

I hesitated.

Sally was all too eager to quickly walk over to the open end of the green davenport and sit down to hear the horrible news. I felt like crying already and I had no idea what I was about to hear, but I approached with apprehension and sat down on the footstool near my mother's favorite chair, where she was once again seated, near the edge.

"Girls," my father said, "there's been a terrible tragedy." Both Sally and I sat up straight, and Sandy's tears started falling again.

"What could possibly be so bad?" Sally quizzed.

"This is not easy to talk about, but Sandy learned this morning that Tom has...." my father's words trailed off as he wasn't able to complete what he was trying to say. But those simple words were enough to cause more crying.

Greg cleared his throat and said, "I'll give it a try." He cleared his throat again, and continued, "This morning Tom's dad found him dead in the barn." I instantly stood up, feeling like I had been punched in the stomach and should run before I heard anything more.

But Sally's words shook me from my shock, "What do you mean he is dead? How?" There was a slow response to her question, causing many things to run violently through my head. The first person who came to mind was a pregnant Jolene, then the whole breakup for Sandy, and Ellen so angry with Sally, the image of Tom at our Fourth of July barbecue, the Vietnam war. I got so woozy with those thoughts that I sat back down again.

Sandy seemed to find her voice and some relief from her tears because she added, "This morning my dad came home from the hospital and told me the news. Tom committed suicide." The news sounded surreal and I was disoriented. Sally was speechless, so was I. Sandy took a deep breath and continued, "That's about all I know."

There was a heavy silence in the room, most of us hanging our heads trying to understand what was going on in the hearts and minds of each other. Rosie jumped at my legs. I scooped her up and hugged her close. She calmed my racing heart.

But I started feeling guilty for not liking Tom, and almost hating him for the mess he caused for Sandy and Jolene. He killed himself and that posed a lot of unanswered questions.

"Why and how?" Sally was demanding an answer. I was pretty sure she was thinking how she was going to tell Jolene in a letter.

"We don't really know." My father stood up, took a deep sigh and said, "I'm going outside for some fresh air. This news is disturbing."

After my father had gone out to the garage, Ellen said, "All we know is that Mr. Ganley found Tom hanging from the barn rafters early this morning. At this point we can only guess why, but who knows for sure."

Sandy sobbed from hearing those words and Greg reached his

arm around her and pulled her into his side. Noticing his kind way of comforting her made me love him even more than I already did.

But I, too, was beginning to feel like my father, and needed to get away from this conversation. I stood up and said to Rosie, "Come on girl." And I headed toward the stairs with her right beside me. Rosie and I went into the closet and shut out the world with the door.

My head was spinning.

I had never known anyone who killed themself. In fact, other than watching the funerals on TV of Martin Luther King, Jr. and Bobby Kennedy, I didn't know people who died, especially not someone who committed suicide.

Ellen was right, this kind of news was going to spread quickly and would be a shock in our community and at school, even though Tom had now graduated.

I gulped. This was terrible for Tom's family and my heart was hurting for Sandy. Then, I started thinking about the times I had read Ellen's diary and how Sandy and Ellen thought he was depressed or unhappy. Maybe the whole situation with Jolene and the baby, the breakup, the war — who knew what else — was piling up for Tom.

I stayed in the dark closet for a while, letting all my thoughts race around until I was tired, but Rosie started chasing her tail telling me we should go outside and play. Perhaps dogs had a better understanding of life than people did.

~ *Chapter 35* ~

Days later, some of the shock about Tom was easing up, but now all of us were going to attend his funeral at Our Lady of Favor Catholic Church. I'd never been inside of that church and wondered what Pastor Prewitt would think of us inside the Catholic church. But, nonetheless, I went along with my family.

It was Tuesday morning and my mother instructed us to put on our Sunday clothes. Ellen was already dressed and doing her makeup as I stood in her doorway looking at her. She caught me standing there, staring, and said, "Anna, come in if you'd like."

I hesitated for a moment as I knew I should be getting ready too.

"Are you okay?" she asked me. I wasn't sure I had an answer to her question. Actually, none of us were really okay. I just hoped eventually we would be. I stood silent. "Anna, come and sit down and tell me what you want to say." She was about to rub lipstick on her lips as she said it.

"I don't really have anything to say," I responded. She looked at me, her eyes seemed sad.

"Is it alright for us to go inside the Catholic church?" I asked because I didn't know what else to talk about. All I really wanted was to be near her.

She smiled in a tender way that I hadn't seen in days. "Of course, silly. It's just fine when it's a funeral."

Her smile made me smile and I asked, "What should I wear?"

Ellen took a deep breath and said, "Why don't you give me a few minutes to finish up and then I'll help you choose something. I will also fix your hair, would you like that?"

I beamed at her because a small act of kindness was just enough to lighten my heartache. But it also made me question my sadness over a guy who was not the nicest person in the first place — a person who hurt others in so many ways. I'd have to try and understand what it was that caused the human heart to break over so many things.

My family, including my father, got into the Galaxie after he backed it out of the garage. The usual arrangement was for me to sit between my sisters as that seemed to keep any disagreements at bay. We drove to the church in silence. I, for one, wasn't sure what to expect. Going to a funeral was a new experience for me.

As we pulled into the parking lot, Ellen asked my parents, "Do you mind if I sit with Sandy? Greg and I would like to be there for her." They nodded, leaving me and Sally with our parents. I had no idea how the Catholics chose their pews, but we'd have to sit wherever our parents directed us. Thinking about the comfort of our pew at Salvation Lutheran added to the anxiety of being in a different church.

As we entered, we saw a black hearse parked in front of the church, and inside we joined a large assembly of people. Some I recognized and some I didn't. I followed my parents to a line to greet Tom's family and view his body inside of a dark, shiny casket.

I was very uneasy and felt tightness in my chest. I had never seen a dead body before. I did my best to look away from where Tom's lifeless body lay inside the casket, but Sally seemed quite interested as she stood on tip toes, stretched her neck and gazed around people trying to see the boy who was once a star quarterback and Sandy's two-timing boyfriend. I just wanted to get to a pew and sit, as quickly as possible.

Once we were through the line, we were handed a bulletin with Tom's graduation picture on the front, including his date of birth and date of death. Something was gripping my chest with enormous strength and I wanted it to go away, but figured I may not be released from the grasp until we were once again out of the church, and back home. The experience of my first funeral proved to be more than I could understand, or process.

I couldn't help notice Tom's heartbroken family; his mother and father and his older brother, Terry, and younger sister, Tammy. I quickly looked away. At the front of the church was Sandy and her family along with Ellen and Greg. I noticed that many people were devastated because one person chose to end his life.

The priest at the Catholic church wore a robe and stole much more showy than our minister, and the church itself was also more fancy. I looked around and found comfort in the stained-glass windows, carved wood and a statue of Jesus hanging on a cross at the front of the church.

I thought about how I wasn't the best Christian kid but to see Jesus on the cross reminded me what suffering was about, and it occurred to me that maybe it was all I needed to know. The word *suffer* was fixed in my mind from hearing it often enough in church, and Sunday school.

As soon as I had this thought, I felt the gripping release my heart. Then I noticed a ray of sun stream through the east-facing, stained-glass window that brightened the image of Jesus holding a small child. It was enough comfort to carry me through the rest of Tom's funeral.

It wasn't until the priest had preached, various people had spoken, and several hymns were sung that we were finally able to leave. This was the end of Tom's life as all of us knew it, but it was now the beginning of the cycle of grief for those who loved him.

Who could truly understand any of it?

Chapter 36

The general feeling of shock and numbness still hung over my family, but it was Sandy who wore sadness like a dark cloud.

A number of days had passed since Tom's funeral and my mother said, "Girls, next week we are going to Mankato to shop for school clothes and supplies. I want you to check your closets for outgrown clothing and shoes, and then make a list of what you need."

It was Sally who seemed to be doing most of the growing these days. I'd get some hand-me-downs along with some new things, but clearly this trip was going to be all about her.

Every year we'd make a day trip to Mankato, which was about seventy-five miles north and east from Springville, for our school shopping, and to visit my father's parents.

There was something as exciting about the first day of school as there was about the last day. We loved our summer vacation, but it seemed by the end of August, we were all ready to get back into the school routine, and be with our friends.

We loved our school shopping, but it also meant that we'd need to have lunch with grandma and grandpa Hendricks, who had lived in Mankato for as long as I could remember.

Visiting them was always the most dreaded part of the day. All of us would groan when my mother mentioned it, but it was Sally who said, "I don't like going to grandma's house." She would make the same complaint every year without fail. "Their house smells bad and they're always crabby." She pinched her noise to make a point.

"Young lady, do not be disrespectful!" My mother scolded her. "If we can't say nice things, we shouldn't say anything." That comment always resonated with me, and so I kept bad thoughts inside my head most of the time. But Sally had trouble keeping anything to herself. And, Ellen had long ago given up any protest about visiting our grandparents.

"Well, it's true, and why do we have to go to their house, they never visit us?" Sally kept on, not concerned about talking back to our mother.

"Listen here, they are your grandparents, and your father's parents, and so it is only right for us to be kind and loving to family, understand?" My mother held firm in her response whether she cared about our grandparents or not. She seemed to honestly believe doing the right thing was the only way in life, even though it often appeared she wasn't exactly fond of my grandparents.

I wasn't convinced that my father cared all that much about his family either. It's not like he went along with us to Mankato to shop. Or to visit his parents.

This year our shopping trip was going to be a little bit different, my mother had reminded us. "After we have lunch with grandma and grandpa, we will go to Mankato State College," she said, smiling. I felt like she was trying hard to move on from the recent tragedy of Tom.

I had to admit, the talk about school and shopping was something to lighten our spirits and I could feel it with my sisters as well.

Sandy happened to be at our house when all the talk about school, and shopping, was going on. Out of the blue, Ellen seemed to have a bright idea and asked, "Mom, is it possible for Sandy to come along with us this once?"

The question brightened my heart as I wanted Sandy to come along with us, too. Even she smiled at this idea, which was good to see after all the tears she'd shed lately. *This once* that Ellen was referring to indicated that this would be the last time she would go with us school shopping since she was going to be a senior, and now we were also going to include a visit to a college.

I had a strange feeling of both uncertainty and excitement.

Chiming in with her own idea was Sally, not asking but insisting, "I want to take a friend, too!"

It appeared to me that she was moving on from her friendship with Jolene. It was almost like she was outgrowing her like some of her clothes. The strain of a long distance friendship seemed to be happening whether Sally could see it or not.

My feeling was that Jolene was being replaced. But, even so, the two were still writing back and forth to each other, and certainly the topic of Tom was most likely enough for the two girls to keep bouncing letters back and forth like a game of tennis. At least for now.

What was interesting to me was that Sally needed to be with people, and she needed her friends. The way I saw her moving on was that she now was spending a lot of time with a girl named Jennifer Jones, who lived on Clark Street, which was several blocks down and over from our house. In the short time since Jolene had left town, Sally was becoming quite fascinated with Jennifer, or Jen as she called her.

Jennifer Jones was a very pretty girl with red hair that trailed down past her shoulders which she would frequently sweep back with her fingers. When she did this, I couldn't help notice the sweet sprinkle of freckles across her nose. It was like the entire gesture was to show off her pretty features with grand intention. Jennifer was fourteen years old, which I knew was very attractive to Sally because she couldn't wait to grow up.

I was pretty sure that Jen was the friend that Sally wanted to take along to Mankato, but my mother's response was, "Not this time, my dear. I think one friend is enough. Sandy, you may join us if you'd like and your parents are fine with it." Then my mother looked at Sandy for response and asked, "Are you thinking about Mankato State College?"

I knew Sandy hadn't been herself lately, but she forced a smile and said, "I think I am and I would like to go along to Mankato, but I'll check with my parents."

"Why can't I have a friend come along? It's not fair that Ellen always gets everything she wants!" Sally stomped her foot, crossed her arms over her chest, and frowned at my mother, as if any of it would change the decision that had been made.

"Because I said so," my mother insisted. Her tone warned us that she was not interested in any more discussion about who was going and who was not. Thankfully, Sally let it rest.

"So now, why don't all of you go clean your closets and make your lists," she stated brightly. I had to admit this might have seemed like work if the final outcome didn't have the reward of new clothes and shoes in the end.

In our room, Sally and I started going through our closet, jotting down items we thought we'd need for the quickly approaching school year. Sally's pouting didn't last long as she said to me, "Isn't Jen just the neatest girl?" She looked at me with a dreamy stare. "I mean, I miss Jolene, but I need to move on," she continued, examining a blouse to decide if it would become mine.

"Jen has such a cool name." Sally threw the blouse on her bed and wrote something down on a sheet of paper. "I just love her name! It sounds so...oh...I don't know — so Hollywood!"

I was stunned how just saying the name brought such a bright, happy smile to her face. It was like she had made a discovery that would change her life. "And, that wouldn't surprise me, you know?" Sally continued to rattle on as if really not talking to me, but just thinking out loud. "She has been in plays and she is so beautiful, I can see her in Hollywood one day, don't you think, Anna?"

I didn't answer her right away as I was pondering how captivated she was with her new friend. I was also sizing up the difference in Sally's speech and actions. It was as though she had grown up years in just a few weeks.

My response was weak as I said, "I guess so."

"You guess so? What are you, blind?" The light in her eyes disappeared as Sally was looking for more confirmation than I was giving. I knew her well enough to know that she had a lovely new friend, and I should be jealous.

"Yeah, she's pretty," I said, though I still didn't sound convincing, but I really did think Jen was very pretty. I was just trying to sort out why and how Sally was changing so quickly in such a short time, but maybe I was overthinking it.

Sally continued sorting through her things and talking as she worked. "And, she is fourteen! I cannot wait for February when I finally turn thirteen! I'm so tired of being anything less, you know? Jen tells me that being a teenager is the absolute best!"

The more Sally prattled on, I knew trying to dissuade her was like trying to stop a runaway train. It was obvious to me that Sally was becoming very enamored with her new friend. I just hoped I could tolerate her.

~ *Chapter 37* ~

I t was Monday afternoon when I came home alone from the park because Sally went to Jen's house and made it clear that I was not invited along. As I rode into the driveway, I noticed the familiar rusty truck that belonged to Mr. Leroy.

What is he doing here? I thought as I dropped my bike in the grass next to the house.

I decided it was best that I slip in quietly through the front door, into the living room, so I wouldn't be noticed.

My father was at work and I assumed Ellen was, too, as the Falcon was gone. It was just my mother and Mr. Leroy, alone, in my house. It caused my breath to catch in my throat.

As I entered, I carefully closed the door so it wouldn't make a sound. I heard light laughter coming from the kitchen.

"Can I refill your cup, Leroy?" I heard my mother get up from the table and walk to the stove.

"I would love another cup," Mr. Leroy said in a low, raspy voice.

I wanted to run into the kitchen to tell Mr. Leroy how unhappy my father would be that he was at my house, and that he should leave right now. But only Sally would be brave enough to do such a thing.

Instead, I tip-toed closer to the arch between the living room and the kitchen so I could hear what they were talking about, and learn why he was sitting inside my house, alone with my mother.

"I have freshly baked cookies, too, and you are just in time as they are still a little warm!" My mother kindly offered.

"I'd love one," he replied.

I could hear my mother pull a plate from the cupboard and then set it on the kitchen table. Then I heard the sound of her chair being pulled in closer to the table.

"I appreciate you bringing the Tupperware back to me so quickly. I guess you were hungry."

"Arlene, that was a delicious casserole," Mr. Leroy chipped in. "Nothing like my Ida ever made. She was a good woman, but she was no cook!" He laughed after he said it and continued, "Nothing like what you've brought to me over the past few weeks. I'm getting a little spoiled, and I hope that it doesn't rile up Ivan, but I sure appreciate your thoughtfulness."

"Well, Ivan doesn't need to know everything I do. I can only assume that you, like all men, enjoy a home cooked meal every once in a while. It's certainly no bother to share the extras."

I sat there quietly, still not sure why this unlikely friendship was happening right in my own kitchen, but it was. I found it amazing that my mother was still so appreciative that Mr. Leroy saved Sally from the river that she continued to cook and bake for him.

There was a brief silence between my mother and Mr. Leroy when my mother asked, "Do you mind if I ask you a personal question?" I was starting to feel uncomfortable, but it didn't stop me from listening.

"Well, I'm not much for personal conversation, Arlene, but sure you can ask."

"I'm sorry to bring it up, but I guess I'm the curious type, since you mentioned her. Your wife, Ida."

More silence.

I could hear my mother sigh, but she slowly continued, "What happened to Ida that night she, um...." My mother stopped talking as she couldn't seem to finish asking.

"I'm sorry, it's probably not appropriate for me to bring this up. Forgive me."

I leaned in closer as I didn't want to miss the answer.

"It's okay. I admit I haven't had too many ask me about her, or bring up her name. I guess it's uncomfortable for others, or they think I don't want to talk about it. I mean, I don't really like talking about it, but......" Now Mr. Leroy was the one not finishing his thoughts.

"Well, I don't mean to pry, I just thought I would ask, you know...out of concern," my mother said, which caused more silence between them.

Then, Mr. Leroy sighed loudly and starting talking, "It's a tough thing. Ida had taken to drinking. A lot! She didn't always drink, but I guess as I look back on it, she had reason."

"What do you mean?" My mother asked.

"Well, several years ago, we lost a child."

I peeked around the corner to see my mother's hand on top of Mr. Leroy's hand. His head was down, and I hoped he wasn't going to cry. I hadn't seen grown men cry before.

As my mother was thinking about the perfect thing to say in response, I thought about the day at the river when Mr. Leroy pulled Sally out, kept her warm and drove us home. I didn't know how his own child had died, but it now made me feel bad for him. His reasons for helping us were making more sense.

"We only had a daughter. Having children wasn't something that came easy for us, so we were grateful that we had even one. We named her Susan."

"Oh, Leroy, I'm so sorry, you don't need to say any more."

"It's okay, Arlene, it feels sort of good to talk about it, actually. She was only four months old. Never woke up from a nap. I guess they have some name for it, but it completely changed Ida. She couldn't get past it."

"Sudden Infant Death Syndrome," my mother said softly.

Mr. Leroy paused and said, "Yes, that sounds familiar. There was no reason or cause. And our life was never the same."

There was another, longer pause in the conversation before my mother said, "I am so terribly sorry. I cannot imagine."

"Well, your girl, Arlene...I don't know." He hesitated. "I'm...just glad I could save her, because God knows I couldn't save my own child."

"Oh, Leroy, stop. We can't dwell on either of our situations. The good Lord is the only one who can help us in this life. I'm very, very grateful to you, that you helped Sally. I think you need to know that God redeems us and heals our hearts."

"I suppose you are right, but as I put it all together, I know now that Ida drank to numb her heartbreak. Her drinking contributed to her death. She went to the bar too much. I didn't do enough to stop it.

The night she died, she was drunk. The car broke down and she attempted to walk home on that cold winter night." Mr. Leroy sighed heavily, and continued, "But she slipped and fell, hit her head." Mr. Leroy's voice was cracking.

I wasn't sure I could sit here listening any longer, knowing that he might cry. If my mother and Mr. Leroy kept on talking, I couldn't hear it because I was too busy thinking about his dead wife and daughter.

He had a real family once!

I was so deep in thought and feelings when little Rosie barked and jumped at me, trying to get my attention. All of a sudden I heard, "Anna, what are you doing sitting there all by yourself?" My mother stood in front of me expecting an answer. But, before I could think of something to say, she suggested I take Rosie outside. I figured she wasn't letting me off the hook, but for now I had some time to figure out how to explain that I was listening to her conversation with Mr. Leroy.

As I got up off the floor and took Rosie out the back door, I heard Mr. Leroy say, "Well, Arlene, I've taken up enough of your afternoon. I better be on my way. Thanks again for all you do. I appreciate the friendship."

My mother walked him out to the driveway and said, "Give church some thought. It's a good place to find peace."

"Thank you, Arlene, I'll think about it. Good-bye."

Now that Mr. Leroy was leaving, I knew my mother was going to ask me what I was doing when she found me on the living room floor.

"Anna, come inside, please." My mother kept on walking toward the back door and I knew I was in trouble. I wasn't thrilled at the thought as I didn't have a good answer for why I was listening to them, except that I was curious. But there was no getting out of this. I had been caught and even though my mother didn't usually get very angry, I knew she was probably disappointed with me.

As I took my time entering the house, my mother was already cleaning up the kitchen, but she noticed me standing there. She wiped her hands on her apron and started walking to her favorite chair in the living room and motioned for me to follow.

She sat down, patted her lap, and said, "Come here and sit." I was moving slowly as to put off any sort of punishment I might be facing, but she didn't seem angry. I hadn't sat on her lap in a long while and it felt that I was now too big for it.

"Can you tell me why you were eavesdropping?" My throat became thick and was unable to answer as I wasn't sure what eavesdropping was, so I asked in a voice so soft, I surprised myself, "What is eavesdropping?"

My mother smoothed my hair and continued, "It's listening to other people's conversation in secret." I could tell she wasn't angry, but I also wasn't sure exactly where this was going. I still didn't know how to answer her and say I was simply a nosy person. It's how I knew everything: Jolene being pregnant, Tom being depressed, Ellen and some kind of pill. I was starting to feel like a bad kid.

"Anna, I'm not angry with you, but it isn't nice to hide in secret and listen to other people talk about personal things, especially adults." I was feeling disappointed enough for both of us. I just hung my head.

"I'm sorry," is all I could say, because I really was.

"So how much of that chat did you hear?" My mother lightly squeezed my shoulders. I looked at her, squinting my eyes, hesitating to answer. "I guess you heard enough to know that Mr. Miller has had a hard life." She was neither smiling nor frowning, her lips were in a straight line and it was hard to know what she was thinking or feeling.

"Yes," I responded.

My mother cleared her throat and said, "Let's not talk about this, especially to your father, okay?" I couldn't imagine saying one word about it to my father. I wasn't about to do anything to get slapped, and I wasn't in the mood to say anything to Sally who would only find some way to get us in trouble. No, I was quickly learning that secrets with Sally was not in my best interest.

"Anna, I want you to know that Mr. Miller may seem like an odd man, but as you heard, he has had a tough time of things. I feel bad for him." The truth was, I felt as bad for him as my mother did. "I'm sure that saving Sally from her incident maybe felt like some kind of validation after losing his own child. Probably no coincidence."

I wasn't quite sure what she was saying, but I did figure she was just being a good person to another who was less fortunate. Unlike my father, my mother was tender-hearted and loving to a fault.

It felt like we both were deeply affected by Mr. Leroy's confessions, but my mother brought me back to reality when she said, "I want you to be considerate of adult conversations from now on, as it often isn't intended for the ears of a child. Understand?" She was so matter-of-fact that I still wasn't sure if she was upset with me, giving me a warning, or if there was impending punishment.

"Yes, ma'am," I responded. This was all very uncomfortable and the fact that I disappointed my mother was enough punishment. I think she knew that, too, because she continued, "I don't want you talking about Mr. Miller to anyone, okay? He told me things in confidence and I plan to honor that. I need you to keep this to yourself." I nodded, intending to keep a promise, because sharing any of it had no benefit.

~ *Chapter 38* ~

I t was now Thursday morning, the first day of August, and we were about to head out on our trip to Mankato. It was only eight o'clock, which was early, but we were excited to do our shopping. My mother had given us about a week to clean our closets and decide what we needed. Now we were ready to go, and just waiting for Sandy to arrive.

As we sat at the kitchen table having our breakfast, Sally was looking over her list. It looked a lot longer than mine, or Ellen's. My mother was sipping coffee and wondering what kinds of things we'd need and what stores we would visit.

"We need to have a plan," she advised. "We will arrive at the mall around ten o'clock and have a couple of hours before we go to grandma and grandpa's for lunch. Because we are going to the college, we can shorten our lunch visit."

Bright smiles appeared on all of our faces and Sally shouted, "Yay!"

I gulped because she had already been warned to be careful about what she said regarding our grandparents. But my mother simply shot her a look that said to *watch it.*

"Okay, Sally, let me look over your list so I know where we should start. It seems as though you've done the most growing." I was sure that Ellen was done growing because she looked like a young lady and was still wearing some of the same things she had been throughout the school year. "I think you all need shoes. It's only right to start off the school year with new shoes." She studied Sally's list and smiled. "What is this about red shoes?"

Sally sat up straight and pushed her hair away from her neck in the same way as Jennifer Jones would. "I want red Keds!"

I laughed as I was sure we weren't going to get everything we wanted, or everything on our lists. She kicked me under the table and I went back to eating my cereal.

"It's what a lot of the kids are wearing and there are really cool colors, too. I want red." Sally was bolstering her case.

I rolled my eyes. I knew why she wanted them. I had seen Jen wearing the exact shoes that Sally was talking about.

"Besides I'm going to be in junior high and I need to fit in." I could see my mother thinking this over, but then she surprised me and said, "I'm not sure that is the best color, honey. I'm not against Keds for your gym class, but perhaps white or black would be more practical."

Sally pulled her lips tightly together, forcing herself to say nothing more. She was fierce when she wanted something. I knew she would have more to say in her favor once we were trying on shoes, actually shopping, and not just talking about it.

Just as my mother started clearing away breakfast dishes, Ellen announced that Sandy was pulling into the driveway.

"Okay, girls, let's get ready to go. We've got a lot to accomplish today, and still be home in time for supper."

Sandy came in through the back door, all smiles. I was hopeful that she was starting to feel better after everything with Tom, though I was sure that her heart was still broken in many ways. I didn't know how long it took for hearts to heal, but had overheard adults say that time mends a broken heart. If that was so, time was moving all of us farther away from Tom's death.

"Good morning, Sandy, how are you doing today?" My mother gave her a gentle hug. "I'm feeling better, Mrs. Hendricks. I think this shopping trip is just the thing I need."

I was happy to hear this because it felt as though we had had enough grief over Tom and, I, for one, was ready to move on, and now school was only weeks away. I couldn't think of a more exciting day, except the Fourth of July, Christmas and our birthdays.

"Well, everyone, I think we are ready to go," my mother claimed as she put the last of the dishes in the drainer and covered them.

Sally was already outside waiting on the step. "I'm sitting in the front seat," she said to me as I jumped off the steps.

"Fine, I'll sit with Ellen and Sandy." I didn't care, because I had to sit in the back most of the time anyway and now with two of my favorite people. *What could be so bad about that?*

We all piled into the Falcon and backed out. Every one of us was happy and filled with joy to be driving to Mankato, Minnesota — an actual city.

The drive seemed to take forever but the conversation between all of us was about the upcoming school year, junior high school for Sally, graduation for Ellen, and college beyond that. There were a lot of big changes ahead for everyone.

The biggest change for me was going to elementary school alone. I was still only ten years old, and certainly not growing like Sally. I felt like all the excitement was held by my two sisters. I was happy, but I was still just a kid. It seemed like it would be forever before I would grow into a young lady.

When we finally reached Mankato, a sense of excitement took hold of me once again.

"Girls, we need to remember where we park the car so we don't waste any time getting to lunch at grandma's house," my mother said, and smiled as she turned into the parking lot. "Remember that one year when we were a little late? She was fit to be tied."

My mother said some of the strangest things, but we all laughed, except Sandy, who didn't know what she was in for.

"That was Ellen's fault," Sally countered.

"Oh, right, Sally! Why don't you tell the truth just once? Being ten minutes late, as I recall, was because you couldn't make up your mind about that stupid skirt at Sears," Ellen shot back.

It was true, the two of them almost never saw things the same way, but I had to agree with Ellen. As always, I stayed out of it. Everything had been going well for the entire trip but, leave it to my sisters to engage in a tense moment.

"Gah, Ellen, you liar! You are the one who was nowhere to be found when it was time to leave." Sally wasn't about to back down.

Finally, my mother said, "Shush, you two! It doesn't matter why we were late. It was a long time ago, but your grandma sure can get testy if we don't arrive right on the button."

Adults had a strange way with words. But she was right — it

seemed silly to argue about something long ago. In my opinion, and maybe Ellen's too, Sally loved the opportunity to argue. She wasn't all that different from my father in that way. She could turn on the charm, but she could also turn ferocious with little reason. It was all too much to understand, no matter how hard I tried.

I turned my thoughts to how beautiful the day was, and our spirits were high as we headed inside. I was so captivated with the mall, filled with all kinds of stores. All we had in our town was the main street, which had separate entrances to each store, but the mall concept felt so sophisticated. It occurred to me that one day I would live in a city bigger than Springville.

It was also part of my parents and grandparents ongoing conversation. My grandparents often reminded my mother and father that Springville was just a dumb little town, and they couldn't understand why my father would have left Mankato in the first place.

It was forever an unresolved conversation with all of them. I would never understand how this argument could pick up where it left off each and every time they were in the same room.

Our first stop, and seemingly most important, was the shoe store. I knew what was coming from my sister. Before I could even finish my thought, Sally was already gearing up for her sales pitch. "I won't take as much time trying on shoes because I know exactly what I want, and we won't be late to grandma's." She was firm in her comment and went ahead to find what she was looking for.

Clearly, Sally was as smooth as my father was with selling cars. She had his ability to sell, whether it be an opinion, a secret, or getting what she wanted. She had a good persuasive case, and the charm to match.

I could tell already that Sally's shoe shopping was not going to take as much time as it was for me and Ellen, but now Sandy was along and wanted to shop, too.

Five females shopping together was the biggest challenge, but we all tried on a variety of shoes, including my mother. Finally, we were equipped with footwear and ready to explore other stores.

It was Sally who bounced out of the store holding the shoe box that contained red Keds! I didn't know how she always managed to get her way, but she did. She never let it bother her that getting her way might come with consequences. She was decisive and difficult to convince otherwise.

To try and understand her reasons and motivation was like watching a hummingbird dart, dance and flutter. There was simply no containing her.

After some time, and several stores, we had purchased a few new things, including material and patterns for my mother. We had looked at department stores and clothing that Ellen and Sandy were swooning over when my mother said, "I know I can sew many of the clothes that we would pay an arm and a leg for."

Ellen was making a case for buying clothes now that she had a job and her own money that she had saved. My mother had always sewn much of our clothing, with a few exceptions. It appeared she wanted to continue to sew for her children.

"I appreciate that you save your money, but it is wise to also save for college." Ellen frowned at this reminder, looked at Sandy and huffed. It was apparent to me that the two friends had their eyes set on having a similar outfit to wear on the first day of school. My mother didn't see it the same way as she continued, "I understand the excitement of new clothes and having the right thing to wear, but we also need to be practical."

Ellen wasn't as determined as Sally to get her way and, therefore, left well enough alone, knowing it was time to move along to visit our grandparents.

"Okay, girls, I think we have gotten everything we really need. Is there anything you can think of that we have forgotten? We can always get more notebooks and such at the dime store." My mother was organized in just about every way. She thought things through and checked off lists.

It seemed that my mother's question was not really aimed at anyone because no one answered, but simply nodded. "Then, we need to get going. When your grandma has food prepared, she is not one to wait for anyone to get to the table," my mother said, and rolled her eyes.

In the car, Ellen explained what our grandparents were like so that Sandy knew what to expect. "They will probably be irritated that we brought you along," Ellen said softly to her.

But my mother heard and, to my surprise, confirmed, "They are often irritated about most things."

My eyebrows arched, and I couldn't help but let my smile swell as I thought it was funny. I had to agree with my mother, my grandparents were often abrasive with the things they said, and didn't seem to have a soft and warm side like grandparents were supposed to have.

The thought caused me to wonder if my father would be the same kind of grandparent. *Who could possibly know these things?* I wondered.

We paraded to the front door of my grandparents' house, and the door opened instantly before my mother could knock, leaving her fist in the air. There stood grandmother Hendricks with only a hint of a smile. "I was hoping you'd get here soon! Lunch is about to be served," she said.

Not even 'hello' first! It was very different from the way we greeted guests at my house.

We walked in the door, following our grandmother to where our grandfather stood smiling. "Good grief, Sally, you have grown like a stalk of corn," he said, motioning for her to come and get a hug.

Sally loved attention and didn't hesitate. Then, he gave each one of us a side hug, when my grandmother said, "Who is this young lady?" She pointed to Sandy, who smiled and stretched out a hand to introduce herself.

"I'm Sandy Hatfield," she responded. "I'm Ellen's best friend."

My grandmother stood up tall and tipped her head to the side as if to size up Sandy, and then offered a limp handshake.

Then my mother stepped up, saying, "Ellen and Sandy are going to visit the college right after lunch."

"Oh," my grandmother said. "I guess I'll set another place at the table then."

We had barely gotten in the door and the tension was already thickening like instant pudding. I found it in my best interest to say little, if anything, but then that was always the best approach to life, the way I saw it.

"Well, lunch is ready and I hope everyone likes grilled cheese and tomato soup," my grandmother said as she herded us toward the table. "Come on now, sit! I'm sure you have worked up an appetite shopping. Tell me what you got, girls."

It was only Sally who was quick enough to blurt out that she had gotten new Keds, but then my grandmother cut Sally off, saying, "That's nice dear, how's the soup? I made it from our garden tomatoes."

Everyone smiled politely, except Sandy who said, "It's excellent, Mrs. Hendricks." My grandma's lips barely lifted at the corners, as if they were too heavy to respond to the stranger at her table.

Then, she quickly changed the subject. "Ellen, did you know that the college used to be called Mankato State Teachers College?" Grandma Hendricks stretched her pink lips wide.

She *can* smile, I thought.

"I went there for a year until I met your grandfather. I had high hopes to be a teacher," she continued. The look on my grandmother's face seemed to indicate that she was lost in her memory for a short moment.

"I recall this story," my mother added, and twirled the spoon in her soup, but her comment seemed to fall on deaf ears.

Grandma Hendricks found her voice again and continued talking about her time at the college. I wasn't sure anyone was really interested as we just ate our lunch, and once in a while someone would add, "Uh-huh", or nod in agreement.

The more I saw my grandparents, the more I realized they loved to talk about their lives and tell stories about playing golf, bridge and traveling.

"Ellen, dear, I expect you will have a very good experience at Mankato State and a pretty girl like you should certainly catch the eyes of a future husband."

I nearly choked on my food because I didn't want Ellen to find a husband at college. She already had Greg, and I felt my grandmother should know that, but I wasn't the one to say so.

Just as I had that concerning thought, Ellen piped in saying, "There is no need to look for husbands, because I am going to college to get a degree, plus I have a boyfriend I really like."

I was happy she spoke up, but still I never wanted Ellen to get rid of Greg and find another boyfriend. That was a terrible thought. Sandy, on the other hand, had hopes of finally finding a boy that was nice to her.

For some reason I felt a strong need to concern myself with all these possibilities. After all, one day, I, too, was going to go to Mankato State College, and then move to Minneapolis. I had overheard Ellen and Sandy talk and dream about working and living in Minneapolis eventually.

As lunch was eaten and my grandmother went on and on about college, her life, friends, book club, cooking club and church, her voice was oscillating in my head, until there seemed to be a low drone taking over my mind.

Then she directed a comment to my mother. "You be sure and tell Ivan that his father shot a seventy-two golfing last week. That will certainly impress him. Is Ivan even golfing these days?"

"He doesn't have time for golfing, like Harold does, but he does get out here and there, mostly with clients," my mother mumbled, looking at her empty dishes. "I'll be sure and tell him, Joyce." My mother tucked her hair behind her ear, and forced a sweet smile in return.

"Well!" My grandmother drew in breath, blew it out, and continued, "He shouldn't have to work so hard. Life is short! I still think he should never have left Mankato and all the opportunities it has to offer."

Here we go, I thought.

"Joyce, we've had this conversation too many times. Ivan is forty-six years old. He has lived in Springville long enough to not want to change his job, or school for the girls! Or sell our house! Not to mention, he loves being well-known in a smaller town," my mother asserted.

I cleared my throat because this whole conversation was getting awkward. I had not thought about my father loving the attention he got in our little town. But it made sense that he and Sally were a lot alike this way. There was no denying it, they both loved being noticed, and well-liked.

The more I listened to adults talk, the more puzzling life seemed, and putting together the pieces could take a lifetime. The older I got, the more complicated it all appeared.

As my mother had promised, our visit to the college was a great excuse to get away from our obtrusive grandparents. And, with relief, my mother said, "Well, we need to get going so we can take in the college and get home to have supper on the table by five. Ivan is a man of habit." She smiled, stood, and placed her dishes on the counter. "Girls, please clear the table for grandma."

We all did as we were told and rinsed the dishes, leaving them on the counter. We knew all too well that our grandmother didn't think anyone else could clean up her kitchen as well as she could.

"Tell Ivan that we expect to see him soon. We wouldn't have this issue of not seeing the girls grow, or not seeing him because he is too busy working to....."

My mother quickly cut her off, "Thank you for the delicious lunch, Joyce. Girls, what do you say?"

We knew the drill. It hadn't changed in all the years of visiting. "Thank you grandma and grandpa," we said in unison. Then Sandy echoed, "Thank you so much Mr. and Mrs. Hendricks. It was nice to meet you both."

We couldn't get into the Falcon fast enough where all the tension went out the car windows and, in no time, we were driving to Mankato State College.

As we drove, my mother said, "Sandy, I hope that wasn't too awkward for you. Harold and Joyce mean well, but they can be intimidating." All Sandy said in response was, "It was a nice lunch, Mrs. Hendricks."

I didn't believe for one second that she really thought that, but now we were approaching the college and I couldn't believe my eyes. I'd never seen a school so large. All I knew was my elementary school and the junior - senior high school, which was nothing compared to the sprawling school before me.

"Wow," I said as we drove toward the campus, looking for a place to park. "This place is huge! Look how big the buildings are!" I was mesmerized, and pointing, as we approached. Both Sandy and Ellen laughed at my comments, though I didn't know why.

"Colleges are big, Anna!" Ellen said as she gawked out the window, grinning with expectation. "Mom, I think we should just park and walk around. We can find the admissions office for brochures and applications." Ellen seemed eager to just get on with exploring. I had to admit, I felt the same way.

I didn't know what was ahead for my sister and her friend, but they sure seemed happy and excited, and I simply felt they were two lucky girls. In one year, they'd be living on the college campus in one of the dormitories Ellen pointed out to Sandy.

It occurred to me they'd see and experience many interesting things and people. As this happiness played out between my sister and Sandy, I knew without a doubt that I would follow in my sister's footsteps. Only, it'd be years before I would be so grown up.

~ *Chapter 39* ~

It was Sunday, and all the excitement centered around school shopping and visiting Mankato State College had died down. Sally and I were eating breakfast when Ellen walked into the kitchen wearing a new blouse she had gotten in Mankato.

"Who said you could wear new clothes before school starts?" Sally hissed at her and took another bite of pancakes.

"Me!" Ellen exclaimed, and went to the cupboard to get a plate. She paused and turned around to continue her retort, "For your information, I bought this with my own money, so there." Then, she casually went about fixing herself some breakfast.

My father came into the kitchen and poured himself a cup of coffee. He was dressed in church clothes, which meant he was attending with us today. He sat down with the paper and glanced at my mother, hinting he was hungry.

I wasn't sure what it was that caused my stomach to do flip flops when my father entered the room. I just wasn't certain of his mood, especially when he was expected to attend church. It seemed I spent too much time trying to predict his moods, or avoid them.

"Ivan, I'm happy you are coming with us to church today," my mother said as she set a plate in front of him and kissed him on the cheek. The thing I noticed about my mother was that she was often so hopeful about people, especially my father.

He mumbled something I didn't understand and continued to unfold the newspaper, drink coffee and take a big bite of pancakes.

I decided since I was uneasy, it would best for me to wait outside in the fresh air until my family was ready to climb into the Galaxie, and take the familiar trip to church.

Outside I noticed that the clouds were light, fluffy, and clearing out. We'd probably be able to go swimming in the afternoon, if Sally would allow me to be with her. Lately, her new friend made it clear to me that I was not allowed to be included. There was a big difference between Jolene Chadwick and Jen Jones.

One was nice, one was not.

Considering Jen Jones had the final say in whether I was invited to be with her and my sister, I found myself frequently sitting alone at the swimming pool. Sally and Jen would be off by themselves, laughing and talking to boys.

Every time I was around Jen, she'd frown at me, stick her nose in the air, and say, "See ya, Anna!" The thing that bothered me most was that Sally didn't object. It was clear to me that Sally was becoming more infatuated, and influenced, by her new, and *oh-so-pretty* friend. I sighed, thinking it was going to be a long school year with those two.

Thinking about Jen Jones caused me to miss Jolene. I hoped she was doing okay. Sally was still writing back and forth, but she didn't tell me what Jolene's letters included. I'd never know as Sally had hidden them and I had no idea where. I had looked high and low, but came up short. It was odd that Sally didn't even share a little bit with me about Jolene. I figured her new friendship was changing her in more ways than one.

Snapping me out of my wallowing thoughts was Sally's energetic voice, "Anna, come on, or we're leaving without you!" My family stood on the sidewalk as my father backed out of the garage. I ran to the car, to squeeze in between my sisters in the backseat.

Inside Salvation Lutheran Church, we trailed up to our familiar pew. But, before we got there, I noticed in the very back pew, on the right side, sat Mr. Leroy. I was pretty sure the rest of my family noticed this too.

My memory took me back to the day when he sat at our kitchen table with my mother, telling her his secrets, and her final words to him, *Give church some thought. It's a good place to find peace.*

I guessed he took her seriously because here he was in church, looking much different than he usually did. His hair was combed, yet he had on clothing that was still tattered, but an improvement. I had to admit, it was quite the sight. I purposely looked at my mother and, sure enough, she appeared quite pleased with herself. I was learning that life held surprises. I just wasn't sure if that was good or bad.

Now that we were seated, we were quiet. As the organist played the end of a hymn, Pastor Prewitt slowly approached the pulpit, adjusted his glasses and said, "Friends, today I'd like to talk to you about influence." He paused like he often did, to make a point. "Let me ask, what, or whose influence are you under?"

My father shifted his weight and sat up straighter. I could tell he was uncomfortable. I was, too, a little, because I had just thought about Sally and Jen. I knew my sister was a person who had a lot of influence, especially when it came to me. I could also see her influence on Jolene who was easy-going. It allowed Sally to be a leader in their friendship. But now I could see Jen taking the lead, being the one to influence Sally. It was obvious to me that Jennifer Jones had a strong personality.

"Are you intoxicated with love for God, for worship, for service, for others?" Our minister continued, "Or, are you under the influence of someone, possibly some thing? Where one has light, the other contains darkness."

I had heard my mother, and others, for that matter, talk about the influence of whiskey. I was certain my father was under the influence of whiskey, and beer. And, because he wasn't sleeping during this sermon, I knew he was listening. I was also fairly sure that Sally was becoming deeply influenced by her new friend. However, I was reasonably certain she *wasn't* listening.

"Yes, it's got a dual meaning, friends. Influence is described in the dictionary as having the ability or power to compel others to act, feel, or think in a certain way." He hesitated again, released a little sigh, and continued, "That's my summarized meaning. Imagine this, Jesus had the ability to influence many in his short time on earth. Why do you suppose that is?" he asked, but not expecting anyone to shout out an answer because he kept on. "Jesus had a mission. We know that, we can find story after story in the bible telling us that."

Pastor Prewitt cleared his throat and raised his voice, "I'm sure you all know that there is good influence, and there is bad influence. Today, I'm challenging you to recognize the difference."

He looked down at his sermon notes and back up at his congregation. Lifting his left hand, he said, "Satan's influence is wickedly dark." Then, he lifted his right hand in the air to match the left. "God's influence is filled with light." He barely smiled while his two palms were facing the ceiling. "The trick is to know the difference, because you can be deceived." He accentuated the word *you* and placed his hands back on the pulpit.

I found it silly to talk about the difference between light and dark, but our minister had a way of preaching; sometimes it felt like he was speaking just to me. Today, I figured he was talking to my father. I wasn't sure if Mr. Leroy's first time to worship was going to make him come back.

And then, Pastor Prewitt reached for his bible and said, "In John 8:12, as we read in the gospel, Jesus says, "'I am the light of the world. Whoever follows me will never walk in darkness, but will have the light of life.'"

Whenever Pastor Prewitt started preaching from the bible, I struggled to listen. I didn't want drift off, but I couldn't help it because the bible was so confusing for me. I wasn't sure what the pastor's message was except there is light and dark, and good and bad in the world.

My thoughts started to wander towards swimming and whether or not Sally and Jen Jones would include me today.

My aimless thoughts didn't last long because Pastor Prewitt raised his voice, and said, "Friends, if you can see the light in the world, in people, or in situations, you can understand the positive influence of God. If darkness overcomes you and leaves you sad, lonely, depressed, bitter, or angry, look for the light, because if we are left in darkness for too long, evil can seep in. You see, Satan is always at work, trying to influence us to remain in darkness, to keep us from light."

He paused again, causing me to look to the front of the church. "It's simple. Being under the influence of God is light. If you are under the influence of darkness, reflect on it. Understand that if you are in God, and he is in you, the truth will set you free. Where there is darkness, there can also be light, because God has overcome the world. Amen."

The service concluded with another hymn and some prayers and then we were ushered out of the sanctuary. But, my father didn't waste any time getting to the car. His body was rigid as he quickly walked to where he had parked.

I figured he didn't like the sermon, but once we were on our way home, he demanded, "What the hell was Leroy Miller doing at church?" He looked hard at my mother. "Hmm?"

"Oh, really, Ivan, aren't people allowed to come to church?" my mother shrieked in response. "I've invited him a few times. From what I can see, he could use a good dose of light." Even I knew what she was making reference to.

"Oh, clever, Arlene." My father turned the car onto Third Street to cross over Main, where we sat momentarily at the stop sign. He looked at her before stepping on the gas. "You know, I don't think it's in the best interest for our family to have anything to do with him."

"Have you lost your mind, Ivan? My goodness, the man saved Sally's life and he's no good for us? Have you no heart for anyone but yourself?"

This was getting very uncomfortable.

"I don't need this from you, I am telling you to stay away from that man, got it?"

"You cannot be serious. I simply invited him to church like I would do with anyone else. That's what we are suppose to do."

"This conversation is done, Arlene. Enough, now. I'm hungry, let's just go home and eat." My mother simply huffed and let it rest. She knew when she wasn't going to get anywhere with my father.

I squirmed in the back seat between my sisters. It was bad enough that the pastor pointed out good or bad influence, and, to be careful because the devil was going to extinguish your light if you allowed it. And now my parents were arguing. I was feeling exhausted and the day was only half over.

~ *Chapter 40* ~

It was Friday and the month of August was moving quickly. I was wishing that I could slow down the final weeks of summer vacation, at least for a little while. But, there was no controlling time, and now the first day of school was fast approaching. I had a lot to think about.

I was sitting in the swing, swaying back and forth, soaking up the warmth of the summer sun. The skies were blue and I noticed there was not one cloud. It was what Sally called the perfect sky because God was smiling through the sun.

It was calm and the air had taken on just the slightest shift that always happens in August, a reminder that the seasons gradually change. This particular morning was special because of that air — the kind that hinted it was still summer, but would soon enough spin into fall. Everything was telling me that school would start in two weeks.

My mind started wandering as I recalled the events of my summer vacation. Surely my new fifth grade teacher would ask how we had spent our summer. It's about the only for sure thing I could count on. That, and the familiar wake up call from my father yelling up the stairwell, "Rise and shine", which Sally was always responsive to. But, then again, she slept sound and hard, and waking in the mornings came easy for her.

I was beginning to feel lonely the more I thought about going to Oakwood Elementary without my sisters. I pictured the first day of school where Ellen and Sally would drop me off and continue driving to Springville Junior-Senior High School. I'd be left alone with still two more years of elementary school. As some things stayed the same, it was the bigger changes that bothered me.

I somehow needed to adjust to being without my sisters at school, and after this year, Ellen would go away to college. Yes, I somehow wanted to control time — to maybe go back to last summer when things weren't changing as rapidly.

Rosie was sprawled out on the cool morning grass after chasing her ball for what seemed like forever. As I looked at her, I remembered I'd also have to leave her with my mother when I went to school all day. I hoped that I wouldn't miss her too much.

The more thinking I did, the more conflicted I felt. I looked back up to the sky for some kind of reassurance when all of a sudden I felt a huge jolt that caused me to grip the ropes on the swing tighter so I wouldn't fall out on my face.

"Hang on, Anna," Sally yelled at me. "You looked so lost, I thought you could use a little excitement!" She giggled with delight at *exciting* me. As she came around the front of the swing to face me, she was beaming with mischief.

"Guess what?" She asked. I knew she was up to something. I also noticed she was wearing her new red Keds. This was a no-no. Our new shoes were to be saved for the first day of school when we'd be scrubbed from head to toe, and sparkling clean, wearing new clothing and shoes that weren't broken in. I thought it best not to scold her.

I worked at slowing down the swing so I could jump out. I wasn't exactly in the mood for excitement or guessing games, but still I replied, "What?"

"Tonight Ellen is staying overnight with Sandy!" My sister was in a playful mood that I hadn't seen in some time. At least not since she started chumming around with Jennifer Jones.

"So?" I was annoyed as I was sure there was more to this than just informing me that our sister would be away for the night. I had been content in working through my concerns and now Sally wanted to play games.

"Aren't you going to Jen's?" I asked. The truth was, I was adjusting to her spending all her time with Jen. Even so, I still didn't like it.

"Nope," she quickly responded. "She went out of town with her family. So, we can do our hair and makeup tonight. And..." She smirked, "we can sleep in Ellen's bed." My eyes got round, as hers were twinkling, thinking how angry Ellen would be if she knew we were even talking about such a thing. But, she was lucky enough to have a double bed and I had to admit, sleeping in her room would be really fun until reality returned to me.

"I don't think we should sleep in her bed," I cautioned. "What if Ellen comes home in the middle of the night?" This had never happened that I knew of, but now it seemed like a possibility.

Sally blew out a long breath. "Good grief, Anna, you always do this!" She slapped her hands at her side in exasperation and resumed, "You take the fun out of every idea I have! They are celebrating their birthdays. She won't be coming home until the morning! If then!" She was right, both Sandy and Ellen had turned seventeen, just days apart, and like every year, they had a sleepover at one or the other's house.

I tried to push away my discomfort with Sally's reasoning. I was also trying to make sense of the mixed feelings I had earlier.

As I continued to think things through, I supposed she was right, what harm could it be? Sally didn't generally think about the outcome of being sneaky, but one of us had to. However, I loved playing in Ellen's bedroom. But to be honest, like most of Sally's ideas, this one seemed to come with a forewarning that sat in my tummy. Even so, I shrugged it off.

With all of my thoughts about school, I now allowed myself to feel excited because Sally wanted to spend time with me the way she used to. It'd been weeks since she wanted to play with me at all. The truth was that lately she had been pushing me away. Everything had been about Jen Jones. All of a sudden I was so grateful that Jen was out of town. It meant that Sally wanted to be with me, like I mattered again.

"Okay, fine," I quickly said before I could change my mind.

"I knew you'd come around!" She waved a finger at me. "Now, after lunch we are going to the swimming pool." This sounded more like an order, but I didn't protest because I had no reason. It meant that I would have someone to sit with and play with in the water.

This was turning out to be a great day.

~ *Chapter 41* ~

Later, we were finishing up our lunch, and ready to rest our stomachs so we could get to the swimming pool, when my mother surprised us. "Girls, how would you like to help me make pizza tonight for supper?" She was standing at the sink washing the last of the breakfast and lunch dishes. "Ellen will be spending the evening with Sandy."

We already knew this but said in unison, "Sure!" We didn't make pizza often but when we did, it was something special. After all, my parents didn't really think pizza was an adequate meal when it came right down to it. We had heard that reasoning from my father more than once. Whether he liked it or not, this Friday night we were going to have a pizza party.

"When Ellen gets home from work, she can take you both to the Red Owl to get two pizza kits, and we'll whip them up later."

My day continued to improve. Sally was being nice to me, had promised to curl my hair, go swimming with only me, and now we would be making pizza later. To top things off, we were going to sleep in Ellen's bed. It was starting to feel like a sleepover in my own house!

After lunch I took Rosie out to play and tried to avoid letting my head spin with thoughts about the upcoming school year. It seemed like my mind could act like a broken record, replaying things over and over.

I had no idea how bad thoughts could come to life and dance in one's head, with no warning at all. I had discovered that when my mind starting turning like a film projector, recent events of my summer would play out like a motion picture. I simply could not stop images from forming, once they started.

There was something about the summer air and being outside with no schedule to get in the way, that my thinking could kidnap me, and transport me to places either dreamy or distressful. But my summer had been filled with things that I couldn't possibly ever explain on my first day of school.

Maybe getting back to school was going to be good for me, I tried to reason. The long school year ahead could lure me away from Sally almost drowning, Jolene getting pregnant, Tom killing himself, Mr. Leroy's dead wife and daughter, Bobby Kennedy being shot just like Martin Luther King, Jr., my fight with Danny Parker, and my bike accident. These were the things that clamped my heart. But, in my young life, I was learning that the heart was capable of moving on and finding some peace. What was more concerning was the mind.

How could the mind ever forget?

Just in time to rescue me from thinking any longer was Ellen pulling into the driveway. I went running up to her like I always did when she came home. She pushed the car door shut and said, "Hi, kiddo, what are you doing?" She kept on walking towards the house as she asked, not really looking for an answer to her question.

Before she could get too far, I told her that she needed to take me downtown to the Red Owl for boxed pizza mixes.

Ellen stopped and smiled at me, then said, "Let me get inside and put my things in my room, and talk to Mom first." Rosie and I followed her. Sally was sitting at the table writing a letter to Jolene. I figured it was a better use of time than my sitting around thinking.

"What's this business about going to the grocery store?" Ellen's voice took me away from wondering what Sally was sharing in her letter to Jolene.

"Hi honey, I hope work was fine," my mother said as she pulled out some cash from her purse. "I need you to take the girls to the store for boxed pizza and some extra toppings because we are going to have a little pizza party this evening."

Ellen looked somewhat surprised and asked, "Why?"

"Why what?" My mother looked confused as she stood there holding the cash in her hand, waiting for Ellen to take it.

"I mean why are you going to make pizza? You know that Dad doesn't really think it's a worthwhile meal."

My mother's face lit up and she responded, "Well, I have a way with your father!"

I had no idea what that was supposed to mean, but she continued, "Besides, things are changing in the Hendricks house." My mother was acting as playful as Sally had been, yet it was unfamiliar to us.

Ellen burst into laughter, "Ah-ha-ha-ha! Okay!" she said, and took the cash from my mother. "And, how are things changing?"

My mother didn't laugh along with Ellen, but she was grinning, and now Sally and I were, too. "Well, we need to have more fun. I've been thinking, after our visit to Mankato last week, I don't want to turn into your crusty old grandmother," she scoffed.

I was stunned to hear this coming from my mother because she always told us to never say bad things about them. This was a different side to her I hadn't seen. To be honest, I didn't want her to become like my grandma either!

But, it was true, we all were used to predictable order. I wondered what other changes were coming from my mother. I could only hope it'd make my father more joyful to be around, but I wasn't convinced that would ever happen.

Ellen smirked and wrinkled her nose as she tried to make sense of our mother, then said, "Come on, Anna, let's go!" She turned and headed to the screen door with me right behind her. We didn't get far when Sally yelled after us, "Hey, wait for me!" Before I could get to the Falcon, Sally was already there hopping into the front seat. Again!

Once we returned with the boxed pizza mix and other items we were supposed to purchase at the Red Owl, Sally and I changed into our swimming suits and soon were on our way to the pool.

I was so relieved not having Jen along with us. It had been some weeks now that Sally and I could be together, just the two of us. I was happier than I had been lately.

At the pool, we laid out our towels, splashed in the water, went down the slide and obeyed the rest periods that happened every hour. As we sat there, Sally said, "We can probably play hide-and-seek tonight, if you want, and watch the stars. I've already checked with Mom and we don't have to go inside when it gets dark; we can stay outside as long as we stay in our own yard."

This was something we could do every once in a while when we weren't in school. The rules were a little looser during the summer and maybe with my mother's new playfulness and promised changes, we could start bending other rules. I was almost giddy at the thought.

The day had already held so much fun and there was more of it ahead. I couldn't thank God enough that Jen Jones had gone out of town with her family. We played all afternoon at the pool and Sally was nothing but nice to me.

I was so thrilled, yet dog-tired by the time we pedaled the distance to our house. When we got home, Greg was just getting out of his car. I had to assume that Ellen's plans with Sandy involved Greg, too.

I dropped my bike in the grass next to the house and ran up to him. He bent down and told me to climb onto his back, then stood up tall and pretended he was a horse. I giggled.

"Squirt, you are wet!" He laughed as he swung me around and placed me back on the ground. "Where's that pretty sister of yours?" he asked.

"I was swimming," I replied. "I'm sure she is in her room. Come inside, I'll get her for you." I realized I was beaming at Greg, who I thought was so dreamy, then exclaimed, "We are going to make pizza!"

"Oh yeah?" He messed up my hair, like he always did, and followed me into the kitchen.

"Mom, Greg is here," I announced. "I'll go up and get Ellen."

I left my mother and Greg chatting and ran up the stairs. I just couldn't believe how wonderful my day was turning out to be. Perhaps I'd have something to share, after all, on the first day of school.

Sally had already bolted into the house and gone up to our room. After all, we had pizza to make with our mother, and couldn't get changed fast enough. However, wiggling out of a damp swimming suit was never an easy task.

Sally was already changing into dry clothes after dropping her wet suit on the floor until I reminded her about the rule of hanging it in the little bathroom to dry. I was pretty sure that rule wasn't going to change. She didn't complain like she normally would.

I was so glad she was in such a happy mood. Honestly, I hadn't seen her so pleasant and nice in a long time. Perhaps Jennifer, or Jen, wasn't the best influence — as Pastor Prewitt talked about — on my sister. But, I wasn't going to spoil things by telling her what I thought. I knew it was better to leave well enough alone.

We raced downstairs, laughing as we stopped in front of my mother. "We're ready," Sally announced.

Ellen was already downstairs with Greg and the couple was about to walk out the door. "Mom, Sandy will bring me home in the morning. A group of us is going to the movie." Ellen was carrying her little overnight case, reminding me that she was gone for the night, and that later Sally and I would be sleeping in her big bed.

"Okay, dear, have fun and be safe." My mother said the same thing every time Ellen went out. Then she turned to us and said, "Okay, you two, march right into the bathroom and wash those hands." My mother shooed us as far as the bathroom door. "And, use soap and warm water," she ordered. I didn't know how much was going to change in our house, but apparently the hand washing rule still stood!

My mother had already prepared the dough, and two round pans were sitting on the table where we were about to assemble our pizza. She brought the dough and some pizza ingredients to the table. Then she plopped a ball of dough onto each pan and said, "Okay, you each get to spread out the dough and decorate your pizza the way you want." Our eyes lit up like a Christmas tree. I couldn't remember a time when we could make our own individual pizza, and *decorate* it ourselves.

Yes, it already felt like things were changing in the Hendricks house and I liked the feeling.

My mother put the pizza in the oven and told us to go out and play until it was ready. My father was out in the garage drinking beer and listening to baseball on the radio. I didn't even care as I was having such a good time.

Sally and I raced around with Rosie, and played catch with a rubber ball that was now losing its firmness as the summer waned. Another indicator that the first day of school was looming large in my small world. I chased the thought away quickly because today had been just about the best day of my entire summer and I didn't want to ruin any part of it.

When my mother called us from the back door, we shrieked with excitement, and ran inside. My father followed us after he stamped out his cigarette.

"Well, help yourselves everyone. Tonight is a pizza party and you can eat out on the picnic table or spread out a blanket on the grass," my mother said in a singsong way. I loved my mother a lot, and I was enjoying this changed attitude in her.

Even my father's reaction to her was softer than I was used to. "Don't mind if I eat pizza out in the garage, do you, sweet thing?" He wrapped an arm around her waist and kissed her on the mouth.

I wasn't sure what in the world was happening in my house, but I knew I liked it. Only, I couldn't see Sally's, or my father's, mood changing for too long. I had to remind myself that those two could be as unpredictable as the weather. I had no idea when my good fortune might end, but for now I was soaking it up as much as I could.

Sally and I ate pizza, drank Coke and laughed. We spread out on top of a blanket, our stomachs full. "Hey, you want to ride our bikes to the post office and mail a letter to Jolene?" Sally's eyes lit up with enthusiasm. I assumed it was the letter she had been working on earlier.

"Is it okay with Mom and Dad?" I asked.

I didn't need any prodding to ride all the way to the post office, but I wanted permission. Adventures with Sally could be a disaster if she changed her mind. But we'd been riding to the post office, without incident, since Jolene moved to Des Moines. Except the last couple of weeks, Sally was making the trip to the post office with Jen, not me.

"Yep, I checked with them earlier," she said with assurance.

"Well then, what are we waiting for?" I asked, and took Rosie inside with my mother.

Sally reminded our parents that we were going to deliver a letter to the post office. We jumped on our bikes and my father shouted to us, "Come straight home after that."

It was common for our parents to keep a close watch on us, and for us to inform them where we were going. Certainly after our incident at the river, they could have grounded us from ever leaving the yard again. I didn't like to disobey, so allowed Sally to respond. "Okay," she yelled back to him. Then, we raced out of the driveway and down the street.

I knew she probably had nothing in mind that would keep us from playing hide-and-seek when we returned from downtown. She had our evening planned so I couldn't see her coming up with any bright ideas that would keep us from going right back home, like my father had reminded us.

Every once in a while I had to stop my thoughts from going to Jen Jones and how I wished she would never come back from wherever she had gone. I wanted to tell Sally that but thought better of it.

We got back from the post office, and parked our bikes in their usual place. My father was still in the garage, still drinking and still listening to baseball. And, I still didn't care what he was doing because I was having too much fun.

The sun was starting to grow weary, hinting it was done for the day. The long summer days were now slowly dwindling and becoming shorter. The colors in the sky were fleeting — swaying and dancing to some joyful tune, unknown to me — and I was held captive in its temporary beauty.

In my dazed moment, Sally said, "Look for fireflies. They come out about this time of night, if at all."

I smiled and said, "Yeah, I hope we see some tonight."

"We'll look at the stars, for sure," Sally stated. "We just saw one!" She pointed toward the sunset.

"Huh?" I questioned.

"The sun — it's the closest one. I remember that from science

214   LINDA M. JAMES

class." Sally was enthused.

We both lay on a blanket, and talked about the moon and the stars. I had to admit that I was starting to feel ready to go back to school again. Our day had been full and now the sky was lovely to watch. I felt peace in this moment, on my back, with my sister by my side.

All of a sudden, Sally was playful again and was chanting the familiar verse, "Star light, star bright. First star I see tonight. I wish I may, I wish I might. Have this wish I wish tonight."

I looked over at her, she wrapped a blond curl around her finger and asked, "What do you wish for, Anna?"

I didn't want to ruin the moment by saying my most recent wish was that Jen never came back to Springville, so I responded with, "I don't know, how about you?"

"Maybe that I'll have a boyfriend this upcoming school year. Jen told me that the boys in junior high like girls much more than they do in elementary school."

"Does she have a boyfriend?" I asked, because now I was curious.

"Most all the boys like her!" Sally exclaimed like I should already know. "She only likes to date them for a short time before moving on to the next one." She cupped a hand over her mouth like she accidentally let out a secret. Then, she sat up and said, "I'm sure being friends with her will help me in many ways."

This conversation was starting to sound strange to me. I wasn't sure if I should tell Sally that I thought Jen was not good for her and would drop her like a hot potato. I looked over at her and asked, "Why do you say that?"

"Anna, Jen Jones is a very popular girl. Look at her! She has the looks, the clothes, and the personality, and everyone wants to be just like her." Sally frowned at me like she shouldn't have to explain such a thing. However, I didn't see the same girl that Sally, and supposedly everyone else, saw. She looked like a snob and manipulator to me, but I didn't say it. Instead, I let those words sit on my tongue.

"I don't know. She just has it all! The boys swoon over her and the girls worship her. She's so lucky." Sally crossed her ankles and leaned back with her arms stretched out behind her. She let out a sigh and bit her lip, looking deep in thought.

"Well, what about Jolene? Don't you miss her?" I asked, trying to make my sister stop dreaming about a girl who was trouble.

"Of course, but things are different now." She quickly jumped to her feet and cheerfully said, "Let's go in and get a snack before we go up to Ellen's bedroom. Besides the mosquitoes are biting me."

I wasn't about to press Sally for information about what she was thinking or feeling. I could see she had as many things to think about as I did. I just wanted some things to be the way they used to be, and some things to change from what they were. Perhaps that was my wish to hold on to.

Inside, we ate ice cream at the kitchen table. Surprised, I noticed that it was already getting close to ten o'clock and we hadn't even done our hair and makeup. But, being under the stars on a beautiful August evening could make anyone lose track of time. My parents were in the living room watching TV and would soon watch the news before they'd go to bed.

I rinsed out my bowl and placed it in the sink. Sally did the same and we both said goodnight to our parents before running up the stairs to change into pajamas. We shut our bedroom door and quietly went into Ellen's room, closing the door behind us.

"Okay, the same rule applies, as always. We have to remember to tidy everything up the way we found it before she comes home tomorrow." I knew it, but agreed, nodding my head.

"First thing is to get the curling iron heated up." She pulled out the device from Ellen's bottom drawer, plugged it in, and placed it on the vanity. "Oops, I almost forgot." She scrunched up her face and set the curling iron on the bed as we had done the last time.

"Have a seat, Anna. Let's do your makeup first," she said brightly.

We opened Ellen's top drawer that contained all her makeup, or at least what she hadn't taken with her to Sandy's. There wasn't anything new from the last time we rummaged through her things, but still it was a fun pretending to be grown up.

I let Sally pull and tug at my face, applying foundation, blush, powder and lipstick. When she was finished, she stepped back, looked at me in the mirror, tilted her head side to side and asked, "Well, what do you think?"

My stained lips dropped open and my painted eyes grew large as I looked like a grown woman in a child's body. Sally laughed at the sight and I wasn't sure what to think. I couldn't help but laugh with her.

But, I lied and said, "I love it, now curl my hair." I wasn't about to complain about looking silly because I still thought I was having one of the best days of my summer vacation.

Sally brushed and brushed my hair. "Oh, Anna, this mop of yours really does need help." I frowned, because I knew I neglected my hair other than to wash it once or twice a week, and then put it in a ponytail.

She worked out every last snarl and picked up the curling iron to see if it was hot enough before gathering a section of hair to curl. Sally continued until every part of my head was in curls, just like she had done before.

"Well, looky, Anna!" Her mouth turned into a half moon. I could tell she was proud of her work. "I might have to think about being a beautician when I grow up."

Sally let out a sleepy sigh and informed me that we needed to put everything back where it belonged. "I'll put the makeup back. You go and wash your face so it doesn't rub off on Ellen's sheets."

"Okay, good idea." I took one more look in the mirror at my colorful face and we both laughed uproariously. Then, I skipped into the bathroom and washed the makeup off with a washcloth.

When I got back into Ellen's room, Sally had already climbed into her bed. I shut off the light and climbed in next to her.

"Thanks for doing my hair and makeup, Sal," I said, trying to adjust my eyes to the darkness.

"Welcome. I'm really tired after our long day. It sure was fun, wasn't it?" I could hear sleepiness in Sally's voice. I figured it wouldn't be long for her to drift off. She could easily fall into a deep slumber while it took me longer to tame any thoughts that would come when it was time to sleep.

"Are you sure it's okay to sleep in Ellen's bed?" I asked, feeling somewhat guilty.

"Of course, and in the morning we'll make the bed and straighten things up. She'll never know we were here." My sister sounded so confident with that statement I decided to not let it worry me any longer. Sally yawned and rolled over.

I noticed Ellen's alarm clock indicated it was getting close to eleven o'clock. I was feeling a little sleepy, too, but Sally was nearly asleep. I tossed and turned a little bit longer before I surrendered to the heaviness of my eyes.

I gently drifted into a dream where I was standing in the parking lot of Oakwood Elementary, waving to my sisters who dropped me off. It was the first day of school. I skipped inside to my fifth grade classroom, wearing my new Mary Jane shoes that I had carefully chosen in Mankato. All the students in my classroom sat on one side of the room, but I sat alone on the other side.

We were instructed to write about "The Summer of 1968". I was squeezing my pencil as no words would come to me. I stared at a blank page while all the kids on the other side of the room were moving their hands swiftly, writing their stories. The longer I stared at the blank page, the more frustrated I felt. Heat began to rise up in me and then my blank sheet of paper slowly started on fire.

The burning paper soon started my desk on fire. I couldn't move. The other kids kept on writing even though the fire spread to the walls. But the teacher and the students didn't seem to notice. My dream intensified until I bolted upright. I was sweating and wondering if I was awake or dreaming. For a split second I was confused until I saw flames shooting up from the end of the bed, and stifling smoke filling the room.

I jumped out onto the floor, nearly crashing into the wall.

Sally was still sound asleep. I yelled at her, "Sally, wake up!" She wouldn't move. I coughed and tried to pull her out. She was so heavy that I could only tug her a little towards the edge. My eyes were burning and the smoke was smothering. I covered my mouth with my nightgown.

Think, Anna, think, I mumbled to myself.

I knew I needed some water. I quickly ran to the little bathroom and closed Ellen's bedroom door behind me, but tripped on a rug and fell on my knees, causing a loud thump. I got back up and rushed into the bathroom, grabbed one of the beach towels we had used earlier and soaked it under the faucet, then put it over my shoulder. In the cabinet I found a bucket and filled it with water.

I was working as fast as I could to get back to Sally. Before rushing out of the bathroom, I quickly grabbed the washcloth I had used earlier so I could hold over my mouth.

In my panic, I struggled with the doorknob, nearly dropping the bucket of water, but somehow managed to get back inside Ellen's room. I closed the door and instantly poured the water on the angry fire. It collapsed, but then a small flame wiggled loose.

I screamed at my sister, "Sally, please get up. Please! Right now! We've got to get out of here!"

She didn't move.

Anger rose up in me and I started beating the mattress with the wet towel. The flames began to surrender, but I still continued my attack on the mattress with the towel until my coughing caused me to stop and catch my breath. Holding the washcloth over my mouth, I tried again to get Sally to wake up. I was reminded how deeply she slept. I pulled at her, but, still, she was just so heavy. I coughed and covered my mouth again.

Now I was crying and pleading with my sister, "Sally, please, come on! Get up!"

I dropped the towel and grabbed the bucket so I could refill it with water when I ran straight into my father just outside the door.

"Oh good God, Anna, get the hell out of here," my father screamed at me. His voice was as cold as the month of January even though the air was filled with hot smoke. Even *it* couldn't melt my father's chilly presence.

He rushed to Sally and rapidly lifted her out of the bed and carried her out of the room, placing her on the landing so he could close the door to the burning bed. I watched my panic-stricken father shake and slap Sally to get her to wake up.

Nothing.

I was on the top stair, paralyzed with fear while my mother stood on the middle step, looking horrified.

"Arlene, hurry up, call for help!" He picked Sally up and carried her down the stairs and I scurried as fast as I could to get out of his way. My father was moving faster than I had ever seen him move. He carried Sally out the back door and laid her on the grass. My mother and I followed him.

Rosie came running after me. I was so grateful the summer heat made her sleep on the cool linoleum, but now she was safe with me in the back yard and I squeezed her tight.

"Sally, come on, wake up!" my father demanded. I didn't know what to do. I was wishing harder than my father that she would just wake up. He sat there looking exhausted, defeated and mumbling over and over again, "Come on, come on, come on!" I noticed my father was panting.

Another couple of long minutes went by before flashing lights and sirens pulled into our driveway. Policemen and firefighters jumped out of emergency vehicles, as well as paramedics who ran to where Sally was splayed out on the grass.

"Mr. and Mr. Hendricks, please move out of the way," one of the men said.

Chaos surrounded us as firefighters unraveled hoses and ran into the house, up to Ellen's bedroom. Both of my parents slowly backed up while the men loaded Sally onto a stretcher and strapped a mask over her mouth.

"Where are you going with her?" My father screamed at them. My mother was crying and hanging on his arm.

"She barely has a pulse and her foot is badly burned. We need to get her to the hospital as soon as possible," the paramedic stressed as they rushed Sally toward the ambulance.

Through a whirlwind of activity, the firefighters came out of the house with Ellen's mattress and bedding, throwing it on to the grass and dousing it with their large hoses.

I watched an assembly of unfamiliar men in my yard, quickly attending to my sister and Ellen's burned up bed.

I stood there feeling like I was watching a terribly scary movie, like none of it was real. I was so disoriented. I didn't know why we had a fire and I didn't know if Sally was all right. I had never seen my father so frantic, or my mother so distraught.

I thought about Ellen and I instantly missed her, and wanted her here with me. With all my dizzying thoughts and the commotion around me, tears started to fall. I could no longer hold them.

Sally was loaded into the back of an ambulance and it backed out of the driveway, lights twirled and sirens blared. My ears, my heart, and my head pounded. My parents yelled to me, "Anna, come on, bring Rosie, let's go! Hurry!"

I started running to the Galaxie, now out of the garage. I had Rosie in my arms. She was shaking, too. The firemen indicated they were staying put to monitor the situation even though I was sure the fire had been extinguished.

My father was driving fast but the ambulance was faster. Once we were at the hospital, we ran inside and to the front desk. "My daughter is here, I need..." The nurse looked up at my father and said, "You are Sally Hendricks' family?" She didn't wait for an answer, but continued, "She is being tended to. You need to sit in the waiting room. Dr. Hatfield is with her. Let me check with him and we'll be with you shortly."

My father's face was unfamiliar to me. He looked like a man I no longer knew. I was afraid. Afraid because I saw deep concern. I wasn't sure what was happening or why, but a feeling came over me like a shadow, and something said Sally was not okay. My heart was pounding fast, and Rosie wiggled in my arms.

It was the first time I noticed that all of us were wearing pajamas. It was almost as if this was the only moment of reality in this horrible nightmare. I was terribly worried about Sally's burned foot. My mind bolted to her red Keds that she was so determined to have. I didn't know what a *badly burned foot* really meant for her. I knew about fires and burns. We had had education films and talks in school about what to do in a situation with a fire.

What caused a fire in Ellen's room? I wondered.

We had also learned about the degree of burns. My mind was out of control about how bad her foot was burned. And just like that, an image formed in my head of my night with Sally and how she curled my hair, then set the curling iron on the bed to avoid any damage to Ellen's vanity. I didn't think to double check if she unplugged it after I had washed the makeup off my face.

Did we forget to unplug the curling iron? I pressed my palms to my head to think.

I instantly felt sick. I ran to the hospital bathroom and threw up. It was enough that my heart and head were dizzy with fear but now my stomach was defying me too. I sat on the cold bathroom tiles and could only weep from confusion, and what I didn't know. I could hear scratching at the door when I realized I left Rosie unattended in my dash to the bathroom. I stood up, splashed cold water on my face and blew black soot from my nose, before I opened the door. I picked her up and headed back to the waiting room.

Dr. Hatfield was walking toward us. And now Ellen and Sandy were running to us as well.

"Mom, Dad, what's going on?" Ellen stood before my parents, her face pale and confused.

Dr. Hatfield placed a hand on Ellen's shoulder and said to my family, "Please, all of you, have a seat." I couldn't help but remember the times at this very hospital with Dr. Hatfield telling my mother everything was going to be fine. He didn't look anything like those other times. "I'm sorry Ivan, Arlene..." His voice faltered. My mother stood up hearing those words, then collapsed into a heap on the floor, sobbing.

"No!" My father yelled at the doctor. "No! Don't you dare say that to me!"

I was stunned and frightened. I looked at Dr. Hatfield for answers. He cupped his mouth, sniffed and tried again, "I'm so very sorry! Sally...." He cleared his throat, attempting again, "She was a fighter, but she was barely hanging on when she got here. I'm sure the smoke was just too much."

He shook his head and looked at the floor where my father was kneeling down by my mother who was consumed with uncontrollable gasping.

Dr. Hatfield tried to soften the information he just delivered to my family. "Sally most likely was exposed to the smoke for too long. Without an autopsy, I'm assuming the cause was smoke inhalation. The burns to her foot were extensive as well. Is there someone we can call? Family, friends? A pastor?" No one seemed to be able to respond.

As the doctor tried to explain why Sally didn't survive, my throat felt sore and my chest was tight. My lower lip started trembling though my eyes were wide from shock. I coughed, and Dr. Hatfield looked at me.

"Oh boy, I didn't think to..." He stopped talking, took a breath and resumed, "Anna, we need to examine you." Fear was invading my mind. "Nurse Reynolds, please take her for a chest X-ray and blood tests. I'll be there in a few minutes."

The nurse offered me her hand while the doctor said to my parents, "Anna may have a lesser degree of smoke inhalation." His words convinced me that I, too, was going to die. "We need to check and then treat her right away," he said with urgency, but my parents seemed too numb to respond.

Leaving my crumbling family behind, I walked with the nurse to a room where she said she needed to place a mask over my mouth so I could have some oxygen, insert an IV with medicine, and draw some blood.

"This will help you to feel better in a short time," Nurse Reynolds explained. "Just relax here on the bed for a while, and then we will go for an X-ray."

I recalled the day I had "pictures" taken of my jaw after my bike accident. Sally's face formed in my memory of that day. I wanted to go back to that day, or any day that wasn't now.

As I was lying on the hospital bed, the nurse drew some blood.

While my body was responding well to the medical attention, my mind was anything but well. Deep sadness consumed me, and I replayed the horror over and over in my head until I dozed off and on.

"Anna, sweetie?" Nurse Reynolds' voice was barely a whisper. "We can go for an X-ray now. It won't take long and then you can be with your family."

After my X-ray, the nurse walked me back to my mother, father, sister, her friend, and my dog, all of whom were emotional wrecks in various stages of shock and sorrow. Pastor Prewitt was now sitting there trying to offer some sanity.

As we sat in the waiting room for any initial results about my health, a fireman walked in and stood before us. "I'm so sorry about what happened," the man said. He was now out of his uniform and he seemed to somehow know about Sally. He sighed before he spoke in a soft voice, "The fire was pretty much contained and out by the time we removed the bed. The smoke is still somewhat heavy upstairs. The windows are wide open with fans blowing smoke out, and we closed the door at the bottom of the stairs." He hesitated and cleared his throat, and briefly looked at me. "We found a curling iron plugged into the wall, and on top of the bedding when we entered the room."

I gasped at his words. This information, and my curled hair said more than I ever could.

This revelation made my family seem to understand the scope of things. My parents and Ellen looked at him and my sister asked, "What about my room and my things?" She sounded almost angry. I didn't get how she could worry about her things when Sally was gone.

"The fire was contained but the bed and bedding were a total loss. The south wall was scorched. The smoke will be cleared out in a couple of days and then the room can be cleaned and repaired. We've also hauled the bed away." He shifted his weight as he stood before us. "And, the bravery for such a young person to fight a fire wasn't wise, but it did tone down the severity."

I blinked away the tears welling up again. He cleared his throat again and said, "I'm terribly sorry for your loss." Then he slowly walked away.

I knew there would be questions I'd have to answer, but for now, no one in my family was asking. Sally wasn't with us any longer, yet I was having a difficult time understanding if any of this was really happening. I shook my head and pushed down the lump in my throat. I hoped and prayed I was still dreaming. That Sally would come running out to tell me that none of this was true.

We all sat, along with the pastor, in silence, for what seemed too long. We had been told to take all the time we needed. I couldn't imagine anymore of this sitting and suffering, but then Sandy said to Ellen and me, "We can go to my house if you are ready." Dr. Hatfield was also there trying to make everything better than it was, and not really succeeding.

"Ivan, Arlene, do you have someplace where you can go? The girls and the dog are welcome to stay at our house for a couple of days, if necessary. This way I can also monitor Anna." The doctor looked tired and ready to go home. My parents were in deep distress and Pastor Prewitt offered to take them to a hotel. My parents could only nod, expressing some kind of gratitude.

I was so tired that I could no longer think, feel or understand how something could go so terribly wrong. Before any us of went anywhere I was given an oral antibiotic, which I was instructed to take for the next week.

Ellen, Sandy, and Rosie and I, slowly and quietly, walked to Sandy's car. After that, the drive became a blur. I had never been inside the Hatfield's house, though I had always dreamed about it. However, it didn't seem to matter as much as it once did.

Mrs. Hatfield greeted us at the door and said she'd show me to the guest room. The beauty of their home seemed like a breath of fresh air — fresh air that felt complete, like wholeness existed there. It briefly calmed me. I had little Rosie in my arms.

Mrs. Hatfield hugged me and softly said, "Your puppy can sleep with you if you want."

Yes, I wanted that, if only I could sleep.

Sandy's mother took me upstairs and I crawled into the twin bed with Rosie. I was too tired to cry anymore. I was too numb to feel anymore, and my head was too heavy to think anymore. All I could do was lie there and ache. But, the bed and blankets embraced me, and soon I was asleep.

~ *Chapter 42* ~

The time that passed after our shock at the hospital was hazy and I wasn't sure what day it was anymore. I didn't care. But now I needed to go home, to the house where everything changed. Ellen said Greg would bring her home later.

Mrs. Hatfield had washed the smokey smell from my nightgown and I was wearing it once again. I had nothing else. It didn't seem to really matter to me. Staying at the Hatfields had been some small relief from the tragedy that was now destroying my family.

"Okay, Anna, let's take Rosie out and then I will drive you home." Sandy's mom squeezed my shoulders and smiled weakly.

As we pulled into the driveway I saw my father sitting in a lawn chair in the garage, smoking a cigarette, staring at nothing. Several beer cans littered the floor near his feet. He stood up when I got out of the car, and stumbled before catching his balance. I hoped Mrs. Hatfield hadn't noticed and I quickly waved to her as she backed out of our driveway.

I dashed to the house, holding Rosie in my arms. I couldn't escape the horrible feeling that his wrath had been boiling inside him for several hours. Hot tears were dripping on my cheeks.

I barely got inside, set Rosie down, when he grabbed me by the arm. I braced myself for what was coming but, honestly, I had no feeling left. No physical pain could compare to my heartache.

"How foolish of you!" My father yelled, as he slapped my bottom. It didn't hurt. It was almost as though his strength didn't match his anger. "What in the hell were you thinking?" He shouted at me but didn't bother to spank me a second time. To my relief he just gripped my arm, waiting for some kind of answer that I didn't give.

Rosie didn't like his wrath toward me because she starting barking at him. He spun on his heels and kicked her. She yipped and ran away. I didn't care if my father killed me, but hurting my sweet dog roused an anger so powerful inside me that I had no way to control it. I balled up my fists and pounded them in to my father, over and over, until I was punching air.

I couldn't figure out what was happening until I saw Mr. Leroy standing over my father, who was on the kitchen floor with blood dripping from his lip.

"What is going on here?" Creases formed on Mr. Leroy's forehead as he yelled at my father.

"Get the hell out of my house! How dare you come onto my property, and into my home." My father shouted at him as he wiped away blood with the back of his hand.

Mr. Leroy stood there with his left hand on his hip and the right one in a fist at his side. I wasn't sure if the two men were going to continue to fight so I scurried over to the wall, and sat, pressing my back tight against it, wiping my tears.

"I'm here to pay respects and this is what I see from the back door?" Mr. Leroy waved his hand back and forth, like he was swatting at a fly. "I'm sorry, but I couldn't let you —" He stopped himself and glared at my father. There was a shift in Mr. Leroy's voice. "How can you do this to your family, your wife, your child, for God's sake? What's the matter with you?"

"Get out of my house. Now!" My father staggered upright, his nostrils flaring, and stood face-to-face with Mr. Leroy. "If you don't, I will call the police." Fear exploded inside me as I sat there unable to move.

"I'll leave, but I'm warning you not to lay another hand on anyone, or I'll be the one to call the police. You should be grateful for what you have."

"What I have? My child is dead! That's what I have!" My father plopped down on a kitchen chair, suddenly he seemed terribly exhausted.

Mr. Leroy just stood there looking at him, then at me, and then to my mother who simply looked like a living person with no life in her. Her eyes were blank.

"I'm sorry, but what happened was an accident. Taking out hurt and anger on others is no way to deal with death. I suggest you think about yourself and stop hurting your family." Mr. Leroy sniffed and wiped his brow. "I'm leaving. I'm so sorry for your loss, Arlene," he said to my mother, but she didn't respond. She was sitting at the kitchen table, but she was lost in another place.

How would we ever survive this awful mess?

Mr. Leroy turned toward the door, and as he was about to open it, Ellen and Greg came in. But he walked right past them, looking down and letting the screen door bang shut.

"What in the world is happening?" Ellen stood hesitantly. I was still sitting on the floor. She rushed over to me and kneeled down. "Anna, are you okay?" I didn't answer, but lowered my head, feeling overcome with shame. "Anna, answer me!" she persisted. Greg tapped her on the shoulder and Ellen stood up. "Someone talk to me. Dad? What have you done, why is your lip bleeding? Why was Mr. Miller here?"

My father didn't like the questions, I assumed, because he stormed out to the garage. My mother continued to sit there as if nothing had happened. I wasn't sure she'd ever be the same.

I could only sit there and cry. Rosie came out from hiding once my father was out of the house. I held her close to me and she licked my face. She seemed to be the only normal part of my life.

Ellen was now tending to our mother, trying to extract answers from her. Greg stooped over and lifted me from the floor, holding me tight. I felt his heart beating as he rubbed my back. He smelled of a fresh shower.

I had never felt this kind of affection from a man. This one instant made it seem possible that we all might be okay, eventually. Greg must have sensed my thoughts because he tightened his arms around me and I felt like I could be wrapped in his comfort forever.

~ *Chapter 43* ~

After Greg and Ellen tended to my mother, they said they were going upstairs to check her room, and get items for both of us so that we could sleep in the living room for a night or two. I already knew I was't ready to go back upstairs.

I needed to go outside. I didn't care if I was in a nightgown. I took Rosie with me for some fresh air and relief, if it was possible to get away from the sorrow that was growing inside my house. I wasn't sure what I was going to do, because everything reminded me of Sally. She was everywhere, but she wasn't.

As I was trying to find a way to escape, Rosie ran to the garage, where my father was. I could hear things banging around. I ran after her as I couldn't trust him anymore. I couldn't let Rosie get hurt, or in his way.

I got to the door, right behind Rosie and I lifted her up before she could go near him. I was shocked to see my father removing every bottle of liquor from shelves and the refrigerator.

He carried bottle after bottle to the side of the garage and dumped each one unto the ground. He stomped his feet and threw bottles and cans until he exhausted himself. He was so lost in this act that he never saw me standing there.

When he was done removing all of his liquor, he sat down on the garage floor, and started crying like a child. I was nearly paralyzed at the pathetic sight. His tears turned into wailing and uncontrollable heaving and rocking.

I couldn't stand it anymore and raced to the secret cave with Rosie at my heels. When I got there, I found a large stick and started hitting trees as hard as I could. I only wanted to destroy something. My puppy didn't understand and stayed out of the way. She, too, knew things had drastically changed.

I wasn't much different from my father, in that, I needed to get the pain out of me that was crippling my heart and mind. I hit trees with the big stick until my hand was sore and bleeding. I didn't care. I dropped to my knees and did the one thing Pastor Prewitt often reminded his congregation to do — pray.

I had always said my prayers at bedtime, but now it was afternoon and I found myself bargaining with God. I pleaded and begged for Sally to come back to us. For answers. For relief from the heartache. For peace. For anything to feel better. I cried until I couldn't anymore.

How we were ever going to be normal again, I did not know.

~ *Chapter 44* ~

The days that followed Sally's death were a blur. Nothing made sense any longer. My mother was an empty shell. She took to her bed with the door closed for several days. No one was cooking or doing dishes. Or living.

My father wasn't much better. He would leave in the Galaxie for hours on end or stay in the garage, though now he wasn't drinking.

Ellen was busy cleaning, painting and rearranging her room, trying to erase the tragedy. I had my closet, secret cave, and Rosie. Not much else. My house wasn't the same. My family wasn't the same.

A suffocating darkness hung over us like a dark cloud refusing to let go, keeping any kind of sunshine from penetrating a heart so broken that not even God could fix. Everything felt empty.

The only thing I wanted to do was make time go backward. I was angry I couldn't change anything. Guilt was strangling my heart. A voice in my head repeatedly told me that I should have done things differently to make sure Sally and I were safe.

I had moments when I was determined that all of this was a really bad dream, and that Sally would come bouncing in the house and let the screen door slam behind her. I couldn't get those thoughts to leave me alone. They haunted me during my waking hours.

But when I slept, I saw Sally. She would be sitting on a cloud, swinging her legs back and forth, smiling as bright as the sun. Or, she would run to the secret cave in her brand new red Keds, blond curls flowing in the breeze. I could never get to her, touch her, or talk to her.

When I'd wake, the nightmare — the reality — taunted my mind to replay the day that had made me so happy, and then so sad.

Days passed and blended into each other, none of them seemed to matter, but now it was Thursday, August 15, 1968. It was Sally's funeral. It was also exactly two weeks since we had driven to Mankato to shop — when Sally was very much alive.

Another lifetime ago. A disaster ago.

Getting to this day only convinced me that we were a distraught family rapidly drifting with the river current, unable to free ourselves from the gravity of damage.

But, somehow, here we all were, dressed in church clothes and driving to Salvation Lutheran Church. My father parked the Galaxie on the street, and we went inside to be greeted by others offering their sympathy.

My family had refused to have a visitation or an open casket. None of it was up to me, but it was best. We didn't need anything more to keep us sinking in grief.

We greeted people inside, familiar and unfamiliar, for what seemed like an eternity. Most of them said the same things, over and over, until it was time for the congregation to be seated.

The funeral director wheeled Sally's casket up to the front of the church and parked it before the altar. My family followed behind, and we were shown to a pew that wasn't where we were used to sitting. It was in the very front, on the left hand side, *reserved for family of the deceased*, as the little placards said. I noticed the church was much fuller than it was on any Sunday morning.

After we sat down, Pastor Prewitt approached the pulpit, stood tall and started to speak, "Grace, mercy and peace to you from God our Father, and Lord and Savior, Jesus Christ." Then, he paused for what seemed a long time, breathed in deeply, and continued to speak.

"Friends, we have come together to reflect on the short life of our sister in Christ, Sally Louise Hendricks. God does not want us to question his timing. Our time on this earth is only for him to know. However, we do know 'A man's days are numbered'. Though Sally's death was accidental, it still is God's timing. She now resides in her heavenly home."

Pastor Prewitt paused again, looking at his notes and then said, "Ivan, Arlene, Ellen and Anna," He looked at us, offering a slight smile, and went on, "In John 14:27 we hear the reassuring words, 'Let not your heart be troubled, nor let it be afraid.'"

Our pastor's funeral voice was more stretched out and slower than his Sunday voice, but he continued, "In this life we cannot avoid heartbreak or trouble. We can only be reassured that God is the peace-maker for our troubled hearts."

But for me, my mind started wandering because my heart *was* troubled, and I *was* afraid. My life was never going to be the same. I wasn't sure if God could give our hearts any peace because we were gravely broken.

The minister said a prayer and then sat down. Greg went to the front of the church, along with Sandy and a friend of my mother's. Each of them read scripture before returning to their seats. It didn't matter who seemed to speak, it was as though everything was in slow motion.

Sally's sixth grade teacher spoke and said things that helped us to smile or laugh which was a welcomed relief as the sadness in the church was beginning to feel like I couldn't breathe.

The organist played a hymn and then Pastor Prewitt returned to the pulpit. Once again he slowed his speech way down, cleared his throat and adjusted his glasses as he always did.

"It seems futile to try and make sense of something that is senseless. You see, there is a space in between that takes away what was and replaces it with what is. It's the space where light falls to darkness, and where life gives in to death."

As I tried to grasp what it was that he was talking about, I heard sniffles throughout the very quiet church. But the worst was my father. His body was shaking, his head was down though there was no sound coming out of him. And then that quiet crying turned into heavy sobs and gulping sounds that echoed in the church.

I thought about how certain things in life are contagious: illness, laughter, even yawning, but I didn't know that crying was contagious until I heard my father's weeping come from a very deep place inside of him. It caused others to cry, too. I saw tears falling on his lap and, without thinking, I put my small hand on top of his big one. After I had done that, it felt like his breaking heart was seeping into my beating one. I couldn't push down the choking lump in my throat, and my tears starting falling, too.

The pastor slowed down his speaking even more, but continued over the sobs, "It's a small space of time that allows an enormous change to take hold. When life is extinguished, there is a grinding of the heart and soul where there appears to be no smile, no rainbow, or no joy; but instead a feeling of hopelessness. A condition to which most people collapse into grief."

Pastor Prewitt stopped talking, and I looked at him to see why. He wiped his nose with a folded white handkerchief, and continued, "Friends, it is my hope that the reassurance of our savior, Jesus, will fill the space where grief creates a void. It is my hope that peace and understanding will come in the form of God's precious love and grace for all of us. And it is my hope that the comfort of God will embrace all who share in this terrible loss. The promise of Jesus claims us through grace and we are his to dwell with in eternal life. Amen."

The church remained extremely quiet as the pastor slowly turned around to sit down. The organist started playing music and everyone joined in singing *Amazing Grace.*

My father's pain and sadness seemed completely drained out from him because he sat quietly, just wiping his face with a handkerchief while the hymnbook sat on his lap, now stained with his tears. My mother had been quiet throughout the service. I had to assume the long days behind closed doors allowed her to get rid of her toxic heartache.

Pastor Prewitt moved toward the casket and raised his hand in the air, and said, "'Into your hands, O merciful Savior, we commend your servant, Sally Louise Hendricks. We acknowledge, and humbly beseech you, a sheep of your own fold, a lamb of your own flock, a sinner of your own redeeming. Receive her into the arms of your mercy, into the blessed rest of everlasting peace, and into the glorious company of the saints in light.'"

The only thing between his words were sniffling and eery silence.

We stood, waiting for what came next, as the pastor turned to face the cross for a moment, then walked in front of the casket and offered a final blessing.

As the service concluded, the room remained very quiet as the funeral director moved to the front where the casket sat. The guests continued standing as the pastor led the way for the funeral director who pushed Sally's casket. My family shuffled behind, all of us feeling like lost sheep. As we slowly walked out of the church, I noticed each pew held family and friends who looked at us with extreme despair. But the one person who caught my attention, sitting in the back of the church, was Mr. Leroy. The person who heroically saved Sally now sat with slumped shoulders and a look of defeat.

Would my family always be seen as broken and victims of death?

We went on from the church to the cemetery, to where Sally was *laid to rest,* as the pastor referred to it. The long, drawn-out process of burying loved ones somehow seemed more like bathing in sorrow than being embraced by comfort. What seemed like an endless ordeal was finally over, allowing some relief to soak into our broken souls.

———————

The days following Sally's funeral and burial evidenced that we were a family who was simply limping through life. My sister had been resilient and enthusiastic, but one of the hardest parts was being in a house where Sally was not, where all of her things were left untouched.

Red Keds sat next to her bed with the toes lined up perfectly to the wall; her bed — empty, her bulletin board with the article about surviving a near drowning, pinned up neatly since the day she cut it out; her bike, on the grass, next to the house.

The stationery she used to write letters to Jolene sat in an orderly stack on her desk. Her alarm clock next to her bed continued to tick; a cruel reminder that time didn't wait for the heart to catch up, but that it removed us from the familiar and transported us to the unknown.

It was as if the deceased Sally appeared to exist as large as the living Sally. Her presence was very much with us in a house where grief filled up the space in between.

~ *Epilogue* ~

I couldn't stop thinking about Pastor Prewitt's words regarding the space in between. He had said, "There is a space in between that takes away what was and replaces it with what is."

I had spread out a blanket on the grass and was lying on my back, looking at the sky. Rosie was curled into my side. It was that time of evening when daylight fades to moonlight. The sky was a marvelous swirl of colors. Blues, pinks and purples.

I could see that space in between, the one where the happy sun descends to slumber, trading places with the moon. I looked one direction where the sun was quietly slipping away, ready to kiss the treetops goodnight, and then looked the other way, where the moon was ready to take over.

The space between life and death didn't linger for as long, and wasn't as peaceful in trading places. One breath was all there was to make a difference.

Sally had twelve years of life and in the space of one breath was gone. She wouldn't celebrate her thirteenth birthday in the way she said she would, suddenly changing from being a kid to a young lady in the space of a day. My family would no longer hear cheerfulness from her voice every morning.

But the most significant were the empty spaces, not so much the ones in between. The spaces that showed Sally had been there were now replaced with silence.

~ *About the Author* ~

The Space in Between by Linda M. James is a coming-of-age tragedy and the author's debut novel. Linda lives in Hudson, Wisconsin, with her husband and two dogs. She has a journalism background, having worked in the industry for several years. A love of words and a lifelong dream of writing a book sprang into reality with this story, *The Space in Between*... just begging to be told.

www.ingramcontent.com/pod-product-compliance
Lightning Source LLC
Chambersburg PA
CBHW070055260626
47160CB00004B/1212